**Gulf**

*From ER drama to bedroom desire!*

Gulf Harbour Hospital has one of the top emergency departments in New Zealand, and their medical staff is second to none. The ER is never short on drama…and when the stakes are that high, pulse-raising desire is bound to follow.
Four medics soon find themselves just one delicious, tension-fueled moment away from taking things from the emergency room to the bedroom!

Hotshot surgeon Mason Ward barely looked back when he left six years ago. So, consultant Lauren can't believe it when he breezes into *her* emergency department looking for a job.

Read Lauren and Mason's story in
*Tempted by the Rebel Surgeon*

Can opposites really attract? ER doctor Kat Collins must answer exactly that when clinical nurse specialist Nash Grady pushes all her buttons…

Read Kat and Nash's story in
*Breaking the Single Mom's Rules*

Both available now!

Dear Reader,

My adopted country, New Zealand, is such a beautiful country, which is why I jumped at the chance to set *Tempted by the Rebel Surgeon* in Auckland, New Zealand's largest city. In writing Lauren and Mason's story, which takes place in a busy emergency department in the coastal Gulf Harbour Hospital, I could explore all the delicious tension and unresolved emotions of a second chance romance.

We've all been young, made choices that have long-lasting consequences. Watching Lauren and Mason surrender to their unfinished chemistry while they try to overcome the past had me rooting for their happy-ever-after from the outset.

I hope you like this passionate story of two contrasting people, each haunted by their former relationship and still searching for the courage to put their heart on the line and commit.

Love,

*JC* x

www.JCHarroway.com

# TEMPTED BY THE REBEL SURGEON

JC HARROWAY

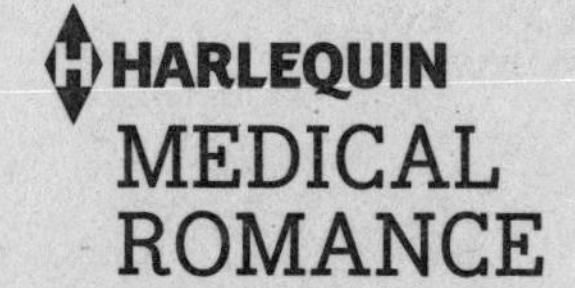

ISBN-13: 978-1-335-73776-2

Tempted by the Rebel Surgeon



For questions and comments about the quality of this book, please contact us at CustomerService@Harlequin.com.

Harlequin Enterprises ULC
22 Adelaide St. West, 41st Floor
Toronto, Ontario M5H 4E3, Canada
www.Harlequin.com

**Printed in U.S.A.**

Lifelong romance addict **JC Harroway** took a break from her career as a junior doctor to raise a family and found her calling as a Harlequin author instead. She now lives in New Zealand and finds that writing feeds her very real obsession with happy endings and the endorphin rush they create. You can follow her at jcharroway.com and on Facebook, Twitter and Instagram.

**Books by JC Harroway**

**Harlequin Medical Romance**

*Forbidden Fling with Dr. Right*
*How to Resist the Single Dad*

**Harlequin DARE**

*Forbidden to Taste*
*Forbidden to Touch*
*The Proposition*
*Bad Business*
*Bad Reputation*
*Bad Mistake*
*Bound to You*
*Tempting the Enemy*

Visit the Author Profile page
at Harlequin.com for more titles.

This book is dedicated to all of the health-care professionals of New Zealand. You do an amazing job—thank you.

**Praise for**
**JC Harroway**

"Temptation at its very best! JC Harroway delights her readers with a forbidden romance and it does not disappoint! I highly recommend this book to anyone who loves a clandestine romance with lots of sparks and so much heart."

—*Goodreads* on *Bound to You*

# CHAPTER ONE

LAUREN HARVEY EXPECTED the same promptness in others that she herself practised. As a consultant in the busy Emergency Department of Auckland's Gulf Harbour Hospital, she was rarely disappointed. Typical that today of all days, when she'd struggled to set aside her personal troubles, the minute she arrived at work brought one of those rare occasions.

'Have the surgeon paged again, please, Grady,' she said to her good friend and the ER's most senior nurse, then inserted an intravenous cannula into the sixty-six-year-old man's arm and attached an infusion of intravenous antibiotics.

The monitor displaying the man's vital signs—heart rate, blood pressure, oxygen saturations and respiratory rate—emitted an eardrum-popping alarm, telling Lauren what she'd already deduced. This man was seriously ill and needed to be admitted for an urgent laparotomy.

She needed the on-call surgeon. Now.

Grady silenced the monitor alarm and adjusted the rate of oxygen flow to the patient's mask and then ducked out of the curtained-off bay.

Lauren pulled up the erect abdominal X-ray on the computer screen in order to confirm her diagnosis: an intestinal perforation. Breathing through her frustration with the lack of response from the paged surgical registrar, she completed the required paperwork. She understood the clinical pressures of this job and shouldn't take out her volatile mood on her junior colleagues. As one of life's planners, she simply liked to run an efficient and reactive department.

Her mind wandered again to the reason for her distraction. Ben, her younger brother, had left home for university in Wellington, not flown a solo mission to the moon. He'd be back for visits. They would speak on the phone. She was overreacting. It was just that she'd been his only maternal figure since he was eight and she was eighteen; it was hard to switch off the caring gene.

Glancing again at the time, Lauren typed up the patient's clinical history and her observations at the man's bedside. She ordered a second raft of blood work, pre-empting investigations the surgical team would likely require. She would give the on-call registrar two more minutes to show up. Then she would place a personal call to them through the hospital switchboard. That should reset their priorities in line with how she ran the department. All junior staff quickly learned that Lauren Harvey ran a tight ship. She was fully aware of her reputation as something of a severe taskmaster, but she was fair and dedicated to patient care. Second to her little family, which comprised her father and Ben, her job was her life.

With her back to the entrance of the treatment bay, she registered a swish of the curtains and breathed a sigh of relief. The flash of green surgical scrubs in her peripheral vision, the vague impression of a tall manly shape confirmed that the on-call registrar had finally graced them with his presence. For now, she'd bite her tongue in front of their patient, but later, in private, she'd have a word with the surgeon about his laid-back timekeeping.

'Glad you could join us,' she said without turning away from the monitor. 'This is Mr Ellis.' She smiled at the patient and began reeling off the pertinent facts required to hand over the patient to the care of the surgical team. 'He's a sixty-six-year-old man with a history of peptic ulcer disease, well-controlled diabetes and ischaemic heart disease.'

She'd fully worked up Mr Ellis for admission. All the registrar would need to do would be to consent the man for Theatre and wield the scalpel. Clicking through the images on the screen, she located the relevant X-ray and continued. 'He presents with symptoms of peritonitis and has signs of perforation—free air under the diaphragm.' She pointed to the X-ray displayed overhead. 'He's tachycardic and hypertensive.'

She sensed movement behind her and, still without glancing his way, stepped aside so the newcomer could access the computer monitor, which displayed the relevant blood test results.

'Mr Ellis,' she addressed the patient, her hand on his shoulder, 'the surgical team are going to take over your care from here. Are you feeling more comfortable?'

At the patient's nod and muffled, 'Thanks, Doctor,' she adjusted the blanket over his shoulders.

'Our Clinical Nurse Specialist, Grady, is going to insert an NG tube for you,' she continued to address the unusually silent surgeon. The specialty was renowned for attracting doctors well versed in taking control of any situation. 'And we'll keep the patient nil by mouth, although he denies eating today.'

She finally turned to face the surgeon, expecting thanks.

'Mason!' The name flew from her lips before she could stop it, before she had a chance to dampen her shocked reaction at seeing her ex standing there in all his jaw-dropping glory. He was dressed like any other surgeon: green surgical scrubs, a theatre hat covering his dark unruly hair, a stethoscope slung around his neck, but as well as the last man she thought she'd see standing in her department, he was surely the sexiest doctor to have ever existed.

'Dr Harvey,' Mason replied with a twitch of his lips and a smile in his piercing grey-blue eyes. The look, which could have lasted a split second or a hundred years, somehow conveyed everything that they'd once been to each other, every intimate moment and whispered promise. But Lauren must surely have imagined those things, because on second glance she only saw polite recognition, as if they were total strangers, which of course they were now. It had been six years, after all.

Lauren swallowed, relieved to find that her mouth wasn't hanging open. What was he doing standing in her ER without explanation, resembling a surf bum not a doctor, all tanned and relaxed as if he'd just strolled in from the beach?

'What are you doing here?' she asked automatically, her feelings bruised and her mind abuzz with questions. But now wasn't the time or the place for an in-depth reunion. Despite what they'd once been to each other, he was just the registrar she would need to put in his place for keeping her and Mr Ellis waiting.

Relaxed, in control and in no way surprised to see her, Mason moved to the patient's bedside. 'You called me,' he said in an obvious and reasonable answer while mirth danced in his eyes. 'I'm the locum on-call surgical registrar.'

Fresh annoyance bubbled in her veins. He must have known that she still worked at Gulf Harbour. He would have been prepared for their paths to cross when he took the locum position. Why hadn't he called, warned her that he was back? Had she meant so little to him that he hadn't given her a single thought?

Lauren cleared her throat, trying to gather her composure while her face burned with embarrassment. Thinking only of the patient and not her confusion and Mason's obvious indifference to her, she made introductions. 'Mr Ellis, this is…um… Dr Ward.'

Even saying his name made her throat scratchy with long-repressed emotion for that part of her past. Fortunately she'd had her family and her job to focus on after their break-up. And, over the years, she'd forced herself to shut down any painful and pointless moments of weakness and curiosity for Mason's well-being and whereabouts.

After medical school, despite planning to travel to Europe together, they'd gone their separate ways. Lauren had stayed in Auckland, lived in her family home and helped her widower father to care for her younger brother while she'd worked her way up the career ladder here at Gulf Harbour, the very hospital where she herself had been born.

And Mason? After his first job in outback Australia, she'd heard a rumour that he'd joined Medicine Unlimited, an international non-profit organisation that provided medical care in countries affected by conflict or natural disaster. She'd forced herself to deliberately lose track of which war-torn country he'd travelled to, which international medical emergency he had followed and finally grown accustomed to the fact that she would never see him again.

Now, for some reason, he was back at the hospital where they'd both trained, his diverse and comprehensive experience and confidence written all over his outrageously handsome and mature face.

In contrast to her shocked and fumbling introductions, Mason calmly and professionally took charge, the way she would have expected from a surgeon.

'I understand you've had some abdominal pain,' he said to Mr Ellis, taking the man's pulse.

Mr Ellis nodded, seemingly unaware of the tense currents swirling between the reunited ex-lovers. Lauren could barely breathe for the pressure those currents exerted on her lungs.

She took a shaky breath, blaming her temporary fragility over Ben's leaving home. It had nothing to do with her ex rocking up looking better than ever, a feat she would previously have deemed impossible. The younger Mason had made her insides quiver, but she was no longer that awed young woman who had struggled to see what outgoing, popular golden boy Mason Ward could have possibly seen in quiet, studious and responsible Lauren Harvey.

In fact, the only thing they'd had in common back then was the mutual absence of their mothers—Lauren's deceased from colon cancer and Mason's had abandoned him the year they'd met, moving to Australia after divorcing his father.

She snapped herself out of it, using her usual rational brain to deal with Mason's sudden reappearance. Yes, she felt ambushed, irrelevant, annoyed that he could resume that professional façade so quickly and act as if they barely knew each other, as if they hadn't known each other intimately, when for the last three years of med school they'd been an item. But this was *her* department, her hospital. She even had seniority, a fact she would reiterate as soon as she could get Mason alone.

Her body heated from head to toe at that idea.

Disgusted with her own weakness, and cursing that, at thirty, she wasn't happily married or living with the man of her dreams, she tore her eyes away from the broadness of Mason's back and shoulders, which were more manly, more defined than she recalled. She had once known everything about him, physically and emotionally, as close as they'd allowed themselves to become, anyway. Two troubled students with nothing in common beyond the pressures of their demanding course and their rampant physical attraction.

'Any vomiting?' Mason asked the patient, the epitome of composed professionalism.

Another nod from Mr Ellis. 'Just once, Doctor.'

With that, a subdued-looking Grady re-entered the bay carrying a treatment tray for inserting a nasogastric tube. Mason flicked him an easy smile and then laid a large, capable-looking hand on Mr Ellis's rigid abdomen. Lauren shivered, discomposed by the sight of his tanned hands—elegant fingers, square nails, a smattering of dark hair across his knuckles—a part of him she'd always found insanely attractive. Especially when the touch of those hands had been directed at her.

She looked away. The last thing she needed to add to today's emotional milieu were hormones. How dare Mason be so unaffected, so blasé and arrogant as to swan into the department after being twice summonsed and act as if they'd never met before, as if he hadn't cared one jot for her, as if he hadn't moved on and never looked back. Not that Lauren herself had confessed any of her own feelings at the time. Then, like now, she'd had no desire to admit to anything so fragile as emotional vulnerability. She was a doctor, had responsibilities. She needed to be strong.

Reasserting her presence back into the consultation, Lauren interjected, 'There's been no history of haematemesis, but Mr Ellis reports two days of melaena suggestive of an upper GI bleed.'

She consciously slowed her breathing, battling the absurd irritation she felt that Mason Ward had disrupted her morning and her ER by simply showing up. She was a mature professional woman, despite the silly misplaced excitement or curiosity or whatever it was fluttering in her chest. Far too busy to have time for any sort of game-playing with this man from her past.

Staying in the hospital where they had been medical students might not have been the most daring or adventurous thing to do, but she'd had other responsibilities, to her family, to the memory of her mother.

Not everyone could run away from their problems the way he'd done.

Mason turned his perceptive eyes on her—a jarring shock that catapulted her back in time—as if he'd heard her uncharitable and unfair thought. She'd understood why he'd had to leave Auckland, just like he'd said he understood why she needed to stay.

'Cardiac markers?' he asked, tugging his stethoscope from his ears, as if he was used to barking out requests from juniors, as if *she* were subservient and he were the consultant.

Lauren tore her stare from his sculpted mouth, pressed her own lips together, lips that recalled his kisses all too well.

Forget kissing, where was his deference, his respect, his decency? Had he lost those traits on his world travels? The younger man she'd known had a reckless streak, was driven but always polite.

Now he seemed far too laid-back, self-assured and indifferent to Lauren for her liking.

She reached for her own stethoscope where she'd left it on the foot of the bed and looped it around her neck. She wouldn't show him how much his appearance had dismantled her, nor would she berate him in front of the patient.

But he could rest assured that there would soon be a reckoning.

'Cardiac markers were negative,' she said, her own tone curt. 'Blood sugars, electrolytes and renal function also normal.'

Regaining control of herself and her emotions, she prepared to exit. 'I'll leave you in Dr Ward's capable hands, Mr Ellis.' She smiled reassuringly at the man who would soon be under Mason's knife. She could only hope that he was a good surgeon, that he'd worn away the chip on his shoulder that came from him being a part of a famous and infamous surgical family. In Lauren's opinion, he certainly had some work to do as a junior doctor in *this* hospital.

She might no longer know more about him than how his kisses, his touch, his whispered nothings had once, when she'd allowed her guard down long enough for feelings to escape, made her feel as if he was the centre of her universe, but she knew that with his confidence and hint of arrogance he'd more than likely made a name for himself overseas.

Too bad she'd have to take him down a peg or two, set him straight on how things worked in *her* department. Despite their past, he was just like all the other registrars in this hospital. Nothing special.

She swished aside the curtain, paused before leaving, settled her eyes on Mason, her heart beating like a rabbit's because, no matter what she told herself, her body seemed intent on reacting to the delicious sight of him. 'Please find me once you've admitted Mr Ellis. I'd like to welcome you to Gulf Harbour properly, elucidate you on the ER's protocols and procedures, now that you're back.'

With her missive delivered in what she hoped reflected cool, in-command professionalism, she turned on her heel and went in search of her next patient.

Every step away from his unsettling presence grew more sure-footed, the memories of them together fading. This was her turf. Mason Ward and the intense connection of their past were irrelevant, despite the fact that, physically at least, he appeared to still possess the skills to be utterly distracting.

# CHAPTER TWO

After examining Mr Ellis and consenting him for Theatre, an impatient Mason left the surgical house officer to arrange the patient's transfer to the ward and went in search of Lauren.

His strides faltered, too many feelings running free now that the inevitable reunion had occurred. He'd expected to see her at Gulf Harbour Hospital of course, but that one interaction had blindsided him, sending him into a spiral of frustration, remorse and utter fascination. An impressive and unexpected outcome considering that he'd spent the majority of the past six years, after finally accepting that they were over and trying to block Lauren from his mind, on an emotional even keel while he'd focused on building his brand as a surgeon.

But the sight of her after so long was powerful, a violent jolt to his system, as if he'd been living in a daze and she'd just shaken him awake. She was beautiful. Whip-smart. A compassionate advocate. And still so sexy that his poor, jet-lagged body was now on high alert, his blood pumping determination through his veins as he paused to collect himself in the middle of the department.

He scanned the staff area for the only woman he'd ever allowed close, and despite his best attempts had always been unable to completely forget, still processing their reunion. Parts of today's Lauren had changed so much as to be unrecognisable. Other parts were exactly how he remembered. It made her both achingly familiar and delightfully new, each revelation unsettling.

He hadn't cyber-stalked her career path or her personal life after their first year apart for reasons of self-preservation but, whatever her marital status now, this unforeseen flare-up of interest in her needed to be nipped in the bud.

It didn't help his cause that she was still stunning, her dark and emotive eyes a place a man could lose himself if he wasn't careful, her glossy brown hair tamed into a practical ponytail for work and her figure a little more voluptuous than he recalled. And where Lauren was concerned, as soon as he allowed himself to imagine, the details came to him surprisingly undiminished.

All that was missing was her beaming smile, the one he'd coaxed out of her a million times, the one that'd had the power to quicken his pulse and pull him out of any funk. Now she seemed all hard edges, checklists and rules.

He sighed; he should have warned her of his return. Now he had some grovelling to do.

He quickened his pace, ducked his head into various parts of the ER and found Lauren at the work station in the minor injuries room.

His breath caught. With her back to him, his gaze lingered on the slope of her neck. If he chose to indulge that particular memory, he'd be able to recall the delicate softness of the skin there, the way his kisses and the scrape of his stubble in that exact spot had made her sigh or gasp or sometimes giggle. The scent of her skin and taste of her on his lips, however, eluded him, and a knot of frustration formed under his ribs because he shouldn't crave a return of those intimate details.

'You shouldn't creep up on people,' Lauren said without turning, her focus on the monitor as if it displayed the erratic and excited trace of Mason's racing heart.

'I was waiting for you to finish typing before interrupting,' he admitted, unable to hold in his smile, because she had always been one step ahead of him, always challenged his opinions, laughed with him when he'd taken himself too seriously. Their playful bickering had been one of the most stimulating aspects of their relationship.

A flood of nostalgia surged through his veins, warm and welcoming. Lauren had been the closest thing he'd ever had to a serious girlfriend. Since her, he'd moved around so much that his encounters with the opposite sex had been purely casual. Until this very second, he hadn't realised he'd missed having someone in his life who knew him so well.

'It's good to see you, Lauren.' Her name on his lips after all this time sent his temperature soaring, as if it were an intimate secret only they shared. Their chemistry had been off the charts when they had dated as medical students, their relationship driven by great sex, mutual support and too many good times to count.

But their intimacies had ended the day she'd called off their plans for travelling to Europe and declared it would be better for them both to make a *clean break.*

That was Lauren: neat, tidy, no loose ends. He'd learned to hate those two words.

Shutting down the memories of how, confused and rejected, he'd taken his mother's lead and fled to outback Australia, where he'd patched up his heart while training under surgery's answer to a crocodile wrangler, Mason cleared his throat.

'How have you been?' he asked. Time to clear the air, dispense with the distracting attraction he apparently still felt for her, so that they could go about their respective business.

Lauren concluded her typing with a flourish, spun her chair to face him and stood, no trace of warmth in her expression. His stomach sank. He should focus on his more immediate, work-related goals rather than flirting in order to coax out the dazzling smile he remembered. Only he didn't want there to be an atmosphere every time he came to the ER, and her welcome so far had been nothing short of frosty.

'I've been great,' she said, looking up at him with those easy-to-read eyes she'd always had, so he clearly saw her confusion and irritation. He had the height advantage, something that had often irked her competitive spirit, but he couldn't help remembering that when they'd embraced the top of her head had fit perfectly under his chin.

'But the bigger question is what are you doing back here?' She placed her hands in the pockets of her lab coat. 'Weren't you in Algeria?'

'Angola,' he replied, stomach sinking with disappointment. He should have stolen a handshake, a legitimate excuse to touch her, maybe defused some of this tension with a mundane professional gesture. Instead, she was looking at him as if he'd crawled unwanted from under a rock. 'Actually, that was several countries ago.'

So she'd said goodbye, moved on and forgotten all about him and everything they'd shared. But then what had he expected? That she'd embrace him like an old friend? They'd had little in common, but there had always been something about Lauren that he found enticing. That hadn't changed.

'So, tell me,' she asked in a cool voice, 'how long will Gulf Harbour have the privilege of your surgical skills?' She straightened her name badge, avoiding his stare, as if his answer mattered little, as if she'd only asked the question to be polite.

Mason clenched his jaw in frustration. He'd obviously inadvertently upset her, presumably by rocking up unannounced. He'd wanted to sit across from her, maybe with a drink, and explain everything properly. He'd just returned home in such a rush and then been occupied with hastily planning a funeral that he wished he didn't have to attend.

The idea of standing beside his father's coffin later this week made him shudder. He swallowed down the absurd urge to invite Lauren along, as if her presence would somehow soothe the part of him that was twisted into knots over his complex relationship with his father.

I don't know exactly,' he replied, reeling from how little he knew of this mature version of Lauren.

Before he could explain his plans further, she muttered, 'Of course you don't.' Something like hurt swept over her features.

He certainly hadn't returned to Gulf Harbour to rekindle what they'd had, but he'd at least hoped they could be civil, put this misunderstanding behind them.

In the same rather clinical way with which Lauren had declared their break-up, she said, 'Well, as you're here now, could you do me the courtesy of a quick chat.'

Mason sighed. It wasn't framed as a question. Without waiting for his assent, Lauren marched from the communal clerical area, away from the bustle of other staff.

So much for the cold reality of his fantasy homecoming, so unlike his dreams of reuniting with Lauren. Mason had always planned to return to New Zealand. Murray Ward's death had merely tightened the time frame.

He frowned as he followed behind her, growing more and more disgruntled. She'd been the one to call things off. Why was she acting as if he'd broken her heart? It was his heart that had been battered and bruised, his heart that had pined for over a year, while she'd moved on.

Lauren directed him into a small office labelled *Dr Susan Wallace, Head of Department*. When she saw his curiosity, she explained, 'Dr Wallace is on maternity leave. I'm acting head in her absence.'

'Congratulations.' Genuine warmth coloured his voice.

Her ambition and intelligence were things he'd found so compelling when they had first met as lab partners. Mason had instantly fancied the smart, serious girl and then quickly come to relish her dry sense of humour and readiness to prove that she was both always right and up to any dare he had set. And no one had worked harder than Lauren at med school, an impressive distinction considering that, when they'd met, she'd still been grieving the death of her mother.

Mason, by comparison, had always felt that he couldn't shine too brightly at med school. He was part of the Ward family, surgical royalty at Gulf Harbour Hospital. If he achieved too highly, there were whisperings of nepotism at play, and if his grades were low, tutors scoffed and compared him to his illustrious retired surgical professor grandfather and his dynamic Head of Surgery father.

He hadn't been able to win. But Lauren had been different. She hadn't cared either way. In fact, the first time he'd talked about the perils of following in some pretty large footsteps, she'd simply laughed at him, told him to pull his head in and shoved a microbiology textbook his way. No matter how messed-up the rest of his life had been, spending time with Lauren had always lifted his spirits, made him feel like himself, free from the expectations that had clouded the rest of his life.

'Take a seat,' she said warily, placing a literal barrier between them as she settled behind her desk.

He declined the chair, cutting straight to the chase. 'Actually, I was hoping I could buy you a coffee.' He smiled, raising his eyebrows in invitation. She'd practically mainlined caffeine as a student. He'd never arrived at her house without a takeaway. 'We could catch up on each other's news.'

He could explain why he'd returned so suddenly, why he hadn't had time to warn her that he was back. Why he hoped they could move past this distance between them and be…friends. If only he could persuade his libido to calm down and see her just as a colleague.

A *senior* colleague.

Lauren pursed her full lips, unimpressed, the move not helping his attempts to forget what they'd shared in the past one little bit. Lauren had done this thing that drove him crazy: talked while he'd been trying to kiss her so that they'd often kissed their way through entire conversations and even arguments.

'That's not possible, I'm afraid,' she said, aloof, as if she had no recollection of ever kissing him.

Mason faltered, wondering, not for the first time, about her private life. She could be married with children for all he knew. He'd have to pump Grady for information later.

His stomach lurched with envy—unless she and Grady had taken their long-term friendship to another level in Mason's absence…?

'I'm busy,' she continued. 'You're about to operate on Mr Ellis, I would imagine. Anyway, this isn't a social chat. You missed that opportunity when you took a job at my hospital without a quick courtesy email to tell me you were back in New Zealand, leaving me to find out at a patient's bedside.'

She clasped her hands under her chin, her elbows resting on the table.

'I see,' he said. Every scrap of hope he'd had for an amicable reunion evaporated, leaving him hollow-chested. She had felt ambushed and it was his fault.

'I've upset you,' he stated. Although maybe she'd have forgiven his oversight but for their romantic past. He didn't want to discuss his father, something he avoided if he could, especially here at Gulf Harbour, where Murray Ward's once prestigious name had finally been tarnished by the scandal he'd caused by sleeping with a patient. A patient the same age as his medical student son.

'Actually, I'm more surprised…and disappointed.' Even sitting, she managed to look down at him with disapproval.

'Oh, no, that's even worse.' He tried an

apologetic grin, hoping to soften her with humour. 'Not a great restart to our relationship.'

'We have no relationship.' Lauren flushed, as if remembering exactly the kind of passionate, flammable connection they'd shared.

Interesting…

'I meant professionally,' he deadpanned, hiding his smile. 'Come on, Laurie,' he teased, hoping to retrieve the playful banter that had been their second most commonly used form of communication after sex. 'I'm sorry that I sprang myself on you this morning, but I do have a good excuse, I promise.

'This is the part where you forgive me for messing up,' he said, trying to draw out her laughter, watch it light her pretty eyes, 'and then we make up.' At least that had always been the pattern to their fights, most of the making-up happening between the sheets.

She narrowed her eyes. 'Nothing about this, you just turning up out of the blue with a tan and cheeky grin, is usual, and please don't call me that.'

Mason winced; he seemed to be digging himself a bigger hole. 'Sorry, Dr Harvey.'

Of course he owed her the professional consideration he'd offer any other senior colleague. He'd once respected the hell out of this woman and still did, despite his bungled return, but nor could he deny that he wanted to smash through the barriers she seemed to be insisting upon erecting.

'That's right.' She raised her chin and met his stare. 'In case you missed it while you've been living in a jungle somewhere with no outside contact, I'm a consultant now. I run this department, and I expect junior members of staff, exes or not,' she clarified, her eyes hardening, 'to present themselves as soon as possible once they are called, to act with courtesy, not make blunt demands for results they are more than capable of looking up for themselves.'

He nodded, penitent, although he knew very well this wasn't about blood tests. 'My apologies. I'm simply used to taking charge of a situation. There's not too much call for strict protocol in a tent in the desert or a hospital basement that's being bombed.'

With impeccable timing, Mason noticed the absence of a ring on her left hand. Not that it meant anything, or that her marital status mattered one bit. They were barely on speaking terms, let alone friends. And now that he'd been forced home prematurely, his plans didn't involve the complication of a relationship, even a physical one he knew would make the sum of all his other sexual encounters pale into insignificance.

'I did come to the ER as soon as I could,' he said, holding her affronted stare. 'Next time you call, I'll run.'

She looked mildly appeased, so Mason ploughed on. 'The truth is, despite knowing I was likely to bump into you at some stage, I was a bit thrown when it actually happened.'

He hadn't expected the visceral reaction to be so strong. At least eighty percent of his neurones had shut down.

Lauren flushed, the colour staining her neck and the vee of skin that the top of her scrubs exposed, luring his fatigued brain to recall every detail of what lay underneath the clothes. How had he imagined that he could ignore this woman who, for him, had always been the epitome of strong, sexy femininity, the gold standard when it came to undeniable chemistry?

*That* most definitely hadn't changed.

Lauren cleared her throat, seemingly flustered by his honesty. 'Well…um…apology accepted.'

With her reprimand delivered, she stood, came from behind her desk and walked towards the door as if about to usher him out. 'While we are on the topic, I'll also remind you that registrars don't invite consultants for coffee. That's not how things are done around here.'

Mason's feet stubbornly stuck to the spot as indignation slid beneath his skin. Oh, no, no, no. She'd dismissed him that way once before, all cold and clinical. Well, he wasn't young and obsessed with her any more.

'I'm sorry for forgetting myself. In future, I'll moderate my tone. You're clearly still a stickler for the rules.'

'And you are still pushing boundaries, I see.' Her pupils widened as she glared his way.

Mason shrugged. He'd rather push her buttons, these days. And if she didn't like his invitation for a harmless cup of coffee, she definitely wouldn't like the hot and steamy contents of his memories. Unluckily for her, she couldn't forbid how attractive he still found her.

She could kick him out of her office—she was, after all, his senior—but not before he'd delivered a few home truths.

Because he was done apologising, and because she kept checking out his physique, her stare sweeping over his chest and lower, he inched into her personal space. 'I can't believe how much you've changed.' The air in her small office was thicker than a desert sand-storm with sexual undercurrents.

Not one to miss out on the last word, she paced closer and quipped, 'And I can't believe how little you've changed.' She tilted her chin, eyes blazing, and he caught a hint of her scent, some sophisticated perfume that a younger Lauren would have eschewed but seemed to suit this older, professional version.

Her stare dipped to his mouth. A small sigh escaped her lips as if she simply could no longer hold it in. It made him forget all about his remorse, the respect she deserved, his explanations. It made him remember thousands of their kisses. Endless touches. The intense connection he'd never achieved with anyone but her.

Before she'd made a choice that hadn't been him.

'Oh, I've changed.' His voice grew husky of its own accord now that they were closer than they'd been since before that fateful break-up on *their* beach. 'The old me would have probably waited for you to invite *me* for coffee. But I'm more honest these days. I call things how I see them.'

An excited flush coloured her skin, the pulse in her neck leaping. 'What does that mean?'

'You and I have history.' Provocation bubbled in his blood. 'I figured we could dispense with the formality.'

He hadn't meant for his invitation to sound so suggestive. He wasn't here to reconnect with an old flame. He had a funeral to get through, a promotion to work towards, his own good name to establish here in Auckland. But older Lauren was still so intriguing, stimulating and unexpected, forcing all his good intentions to the back of his mind.

Her eyes danced between his as if searching, reacquainting, assessing. She was clearly not as immune to him, as uptight and coolly professional as she'd have him believe. Then her stare turned defiant. 'I'm afraid that I'm going to have to insist on the formality, Dr Ward.'

'That's fine by me, Dr Harvey. My invitation to coffee was purely a gesture of professional politeness.'

*Liar.*

'As is my refusal.' She loitered near her desk, arms crossed defensively over her chest.

'Okay then.' Mason raised his hands in surrender. 'I understand. I didn't realise that you still had unresolved feelings for me.'

Her outraged gaze clashed with his. 'Unresolved feelings? Don't be ridiculous. I've hardly given you a thought since you left.'

Oh, that had the potential to sting, if only her protestations were a little less vehement. If only she wasn't looking at him as if she wanted to know more than where he'd been working and why he was back. He remembered that look in her eyes: need.

He nodded. 'Why else would you be so… hostile, so uptight towards me?'

Although behaving wildly inappropriately, Mason was starting to enjoy himself. And so was Lauren. The door was still closed and her eyes shone with the challenge.

'Uptight?' Her jaw dropped.

He nodded, adamant. 'Don't forget, Laurie, it was you who dumped me.'

She huffed in disbelief. 'And you scarpered overseas as quickly as you could, if I recall, never to return.' She straightened her spine, trying to seem composed when her pupils were deep black pools of excitement and her breaths gusted past her parted lips.

'Beyond ensuring that my ER is run to the highest standards,' she added, clearing her throat, 'I have no more interest in you than I do any other doctor here.'

He clasped his chest, staggering back a pace as if mortally wounded by her cutting admission. Then he straightened, his eyes boring into hers. 'That's a real shame because, despite you reneging on our plans, despite you practically shoving me onto the plane with a casual *Have a nice life,* I've thought about you. A. Lot.'

He let the innuendo settle. She might want nothing to do with him, she might be in charge here, might want to control everything that happened in the ER, but she couldn't dictate the nature of his thoughts or the red-blooded reactions of his body.

She stared, open mouthed, for a handful of seconds, as if she couldn't believe his audacity, but her eyes gleamed with fire, showing glimpses of the passionate woman who'd once craved him as much as he'd craved her.

'Just because we were pretty good together in the sex department, don't think for one second that your return means we'll be picking up where we left off,' she blustered behind a calm façade. 'I have other priorities now.'

Why, oh, why did she have to go and say that their sex life had been amazing? As it was, he was struggling to remember why he was here, the sight of her, the sexually charged standoff, the banter back and forth so unexpectedly distracting, so blood-stirring.

He held up his hands, palms out. 'Whoa,

who said anything about us jumping back into bed? Wait, are you saying that you're too busy for sex these days?' He made a tutting sound. He shouldn't enjoy their verbal sparring, but he couldn't help himself. It reminded him of their endless debates over everything from global warming to beer versus wine.

'You're deluded.' She ignored him, this time swinging the door wide open, her intention clear.

He'd finally outstayed his welcome. He'd got under her skin just like she'd wormed under his, reminding him why they'd always worked so well together as a couple. Why they still could if either of them were so inclined. But it was clear that his absence had not made her heart grow fonder, and that suited him just fine because, unlike the younger version of the man she had dumped, Mason no longer sought the approval of others.

He stepped into the doorway, faced her, stared.

'Goodbye, Dr Ward.' She'd clearly meant to sound haughty and dismissive, but Mason couldn't resist one last provocation.

He smiled wide. 'I've missed this. The banter. The way an hour spent in your company seemed to shut out the noise of the world. We had so many good times.'

To his delight, Lauren cracked, her lips twitching, before her eyes rolled in mock disgust. 'I dare say we did in the way a young couple of twenty-somethings can.' She composed herself, growing serious once more. 'But we've grown up. I'm concentrating on building my career now.'

'As am I.' That had always been his motivation for every decision he made, including leaving New Zealand. Leaving her. Overseas, he was just Mason Ward, a name that, to his relief, meant only what *he'd* made it.

'Well, I doubt you'll be around long. I hear that they're desperate for hospital staff in Toruva,' she said, naming the Pacific Island recently ravaged by Cyclone Delilah.

Six months ago she'd have been spot-on with her observation. He hadn't been quite ready to return to New Zealand until circumstances had forced his hand. But now, with the right job on the horizon, he had a real opportunity to make his own name here in Auckland, to prove that, despite the expectations of the past and the impossible standards once set by his father, he was a good surgeon.

He passed over the threshold, throwing out what he needed to say in order to avoid future professional clashes, the last thing he wanted with Lauren. 'I'm thinking of sticking around for a while, actually.'

Shock sharpened her glare as she clutched the open door in a white-knuckled grip. 'Why? Whatever could GHH have to offer an adventurer like you?'

'Don't look so appalled. Is it so terrible a concept that we're to be colleagues?'

She huffed. 'For now.'

With their reunion over, he unexpectedly had no desire to be anywhere else. 'Or for many years to come.'

She frowned, confused.

Mason filled her in. 'If I'm successful in my application for the newest surgical consultant post here at Gulf Harbour, we'll be seeing a whole lot more of each other, Dr Harvey. As equals.'

And now they'd reconnected, now that he knew the sparks were there, hotter than ever, he was looking forward to each and every one of their interactions.

His statement left her speechless, a rare sight indeed.

'Admit it, Lauren,' he said in a low voice. 'You've missed me.'

He left her with a final smile and a cheeky wink, her flabbergasted stare burning into his back.

# CHAPTER THREE

GRADY, WHO OFTEN gave Lauren a lift to work when they happened to share a night shift, parked his car in the staff car park five spaces from Mason's distinctive motorbike and switched off the engine. Relief and trepidation that Mason hadn't yet left work for the day churned in Lauren's stomach. She couldn't avoid him even if she wanted to, so it was better to end this…thing between them once and for all.

She undid her seatbelt and fought the temptation to check her reflection in the rear-view mirror, taking full responsibility for her part in the flirtatious showdown that had transpired in her office yesterday. Clearly her libido didn't care how heartbroken she'd been after her last encounter with Mason Ward.

'You go inside,' she said to Grady, reaching for the door handle, preparing to exit the car. 'I won't be far behind you.' She'd confront

Mason, say what she had to say and start her shift as if he'd never returned.

Grady's stare was laced with concern. 'Lauren—'

'Don't, Grady,' she warned with a shake of her head. She didn't want to hear her friend's opinion on Mason's reappearance. She wasn't interested if every female staff member of the hospital was swooning over him already—apparently he'd already earned himself the nickname Blade of Glory. She definitely didn't want to hear Grady talk her into or out of her course of action.

'I just need to talk to our newest surgical colleague. It won't take long.' She shot him a grateful smile, his calm, unflappable presence as soothing as always.

'Okay,' he said, and pressed his lips together. Then he sighed. 'I won't ask you how you're feeling about him working here. But I'm giving you fair warning—I'll struggle to stay quiet if he hurts you again.'

Lauren swallowed, her throat tight as she tried to keep her expression stoic, while memories flayed her: her mum, Mason, Ben. Before she'd ended things with Mason, she'd been torn in so many directions she hadn't known what to do for the best.

'I appreciate your concern, as always...'

She'd known Nash Grady since her medical student days, when he'd literally taken pity on her one night. She hadn't been able to obtain venous access on a patient and had been on the verge of tears at the man's pincushion arms, when Grady had come to her rescue.

'But I simply need to have a professional conversation with Dr Ward, nothing else. You know me—I don't let anyone close enough to hurt me.' And she and Mason had already proved beyond all doubt that they were too different. He'd gadded around the globe and she'd stayed here, licked her wounds, tried to do the right thing for all concerned.

Sympathy clouded Grady's eyes and Lauren looked away. He'd been there to witness the fallout of that fateful decision she'd made six years ago. He'd picked up the pieces, literally holding her while she'd sobbed all over his uniform, her overwhelming hurt that their relationship was over matched only by the confusion and doubt she'd felt in being the one to end it. Without probing for details, Grady had turned up on her doorstep every evening for a month after Mason had left, never arriving empty-handed. He'd brought ice cream and tissues and listened while Lauren endlessly second-guessed her choice to say goodbye to Mason and stay to support her little family.

Talk about being caught between a rock and a hard place… Of course Mason must have been disappointed, but it hadn't really been any choice at all. Not for Lauren, whose grief over her mother's death had still influenced all of her decisions.

She glanced at the staff entrance at the back of the hospital, her heart climbing into her throat as Mason emerged and headed towards his motorbike. She stiffened. She'd been dreading this meeting since she'd opened her eyes that morning, the shock of seeing him at the hospital yesterday a fresh and startling reminder of his power to leave her both rattled and utterly turned on, for all her tough talk.

Not to mention infuriated. He'd waltzed into her hospital without warning. He'd deliberately riled her up and then he'd completely derailed her day with his revelation that he planned to stay at Gulf Harbour long-term.

Restless, she climbed from the car, vaguely aware of Grady discreetly locking up and heading for the entrance as she kept her focus on Mason and his long strides. She shuddered, her body ravaged by a jarring mix of déjà vu and desire as she watched his approach.

Why was he back? The Mason who'd left six years ago had been desperate to get away from the role he was forced to adopt in Auckland, desperate to be anywhere where he wasn't known, where he could make his own mark without speculation that he was any relation to Isaac Ward or, worse, Murray Ward.

Why had he applied for this particular consultant job? The timing couldn't be more inconvenient for Lauren when she needed all of her spare energy now that Ben had left home to focus on her own career goals—goals she'd already sidelined for years in order to spend more time at home with her brother.

She closed her eyes for a second's reprieve from the sight of Mason, but that simply conjured a memory of last night's dream. It had started out true to real events, her breaking things off with him on their beach, but then it had morphed into a chase scenario, where she'd literally run along the tarmac of the runway behind Mason's departing plane to tell him that she'd changed her mind. Of course she hadn't been able to catch up with the jet, waking with a sickening start instead. Not even recalling the sexy gleam in his eyes yesterday, the familiar Mason scent of his skin or the sexual tension that had clawed at her until she'd been lured into a dangerous game of verbal sparring in her office had been able to dispel the anguished hangover from her nightmare.

Now, just like six years ago, and too many other times to count, she wished that her mother was alive to offer sympathy and sage advice and, if all else failed, comforting hugs.

As Mason reached his renovated vintage Enfield, a backpack slung over one shoulder and his motorbike helmet under the other arm, Lauren stepped closer. She hadn't been able to believe that he still rode it, but his means of transportation was easily identifiable for anyone who knew him well, and more times than she cared to remember she'd loved riding pillion with him, her heart in her throat and a death grip on his waist.

Oh, how she'd trusted him then, believed that she was safe with him, at least physically. Emotionally she hadn't been that vulnerable with anyone. Her mother's death had taught her the benefits of emotional withdrawal in keeping her feelings protected.

Mason caught sight of her, faltered, then the confident smile that spread over his handsome face snatched at her breath the way it had when she'd first laid eyes on him at med school. Even tired from a night on call, he still made her pulse skitter. Blood whooshed through her head with foolish and misplaced excitement. He still had the power to discombobulate her with one look. Nor was it fair that his attractiveness, divine body and sharp intelligence made the rest of the human race look like a bunch of sad underachievers.

He was even a nice guy, for goodness' sake.

Abandoning her membership of the Mason Fan Club, she tilted her head towards the sleek black and chrome machine. 'Still riding around on a deathtrap, I see.'

Clearly her frayed nerves were in control of her speech, the delivered trite observation not what she'd planned to say at all. But, unlike yesterday, when his unannounced arrival had caught her off-guard, when he'd had the last word, she was there to set him straight. Them being anything other than polite work colleagues was not an option. It turned out Dr Wallace was enjoying motherhood too much and had decided to resign, and Lauren had strived too hard for too long for the permanent promotion in her sights: that of Head of the ER. She'd convey her message to Mason, ensure that he understood her boundaries and then try to forget that he was back.

There could be no more bickering. No flirtatious goading. No more talk of sex, past or future.

He shrugged, his fatigued but riveting grey-blue eyes reserved. She couldn't blame him after her tepid…no, outright rude welcome yesterday. It was a poor excuse, but she'd been completely overwhelmed.

'She's a classic.' He glanced lovingly at his bike, even stroked the leather seat. 'She's been in storage for six years and she still runs like a dream.'

Lauren stiffened, absorbing the twinge of jealousy. How could she be envious of a motorbike? He'd once looked at her with similar adoration, caressed her body as lovingly.

'I wanted to catch you before you headed home,' she said, pulling herself together. No more dwelling on the past or focusing on their attraction. With Ben at university, this was her time to concentrate one hundred percent on her career. She deserved it. That left no room in her life for…distractions. And unlike the sensible, busy professional men she occasionally dated, Mason was a definite distraction. More like an imminent heart attack: risky, dangerous and impossible to ignore.

He narrowed his gaze, a newly constructed wall around him since their altercation. 'Did you come to invite me for that coffee? I've been awake all night,' he continued. 'We had a multiple casualty MVA come in in the early hours, but I'm still jet-lagged, so I could rally myself, I guess. I see The Har-Bar is still there,' he said about their once favourite watering hole, a place where they had kissed, danced, argued and celebrated.

Lauren hadn't been there in years, since she'd last gone with him, in fact. She winced. 'I didn't come to invite you for coffee. I'm working the late shift,' she said, genuine regret stuck in her throat for the way she'd behaved the day before. She wasn't blaming him for her attitude, but Mason had always brought out sides of her personality that no one else could, from the daredevil willing to sit behind him on his deathtrap to the young woman scared to risk building a relationship after losing her mother, who had once nonetheless embarked on something wild and passionate and intense with him.

'Of course you didn't,' he said with a casual shrug that reminded Lauren that not much fazed Mason. 'Don't worry; I heard the message loud and clear yesterday.'

Had he? Lauren had been so thrown by his appearance and the lingering undercurrents of their chemistry she wasn't sure how much sense she'd made. That was why she needed to set the record straight.

'And yet you turned on the charm offensive anyway,' she said, her irritation at his calm, unaffected attitude building. The more reasonable he acted, the snippier she became. Maybe because a perverse part of her craved his flirtatious efforts. It showed he cared a little.

He shrugged. 'What can I say? You're looking good, Laurie. Really good. I hope for your sake it means that you're happy.'

Heat fizzed through her veins at his compliment, only to be dashed by the question in his eyes. What he was actually asking was if she'd found contentment, come to terms at last with the loss of her mother, and for that she had no easy, sanitised answer. But maybe he deserved more than *I'm fine*. After all, he had supported her through the better part of her grief while they'd been together.

'That's why I'm here, actually. I came to apologise for yesterday. I might have overreacted. You caught me totally by surprise, just walking into the ER like that, and I was already having a bad day.'

Concern pinched his eyebrows together in a frown, his stare searching in that way that had always made her feel as if he could read all of her secrets. 'I'm sorry too. I really hadn't intended to ambush you. I only landed in the country on Sunday and time just…got away from me.'

Lauren shook her head, batting away his apology; she understood the pressures of their career. 'I wasn't just unsettled by you. Ben left home last weekend.' She exhaled on a rush, as if the faster she said the words the more used to them she would become. 'I was…missing him.'

She'd had no intention of confiding such a personal matter to Mason of all people, but the words just tumbled out, perhaps because he knew Ben, had taught him to surf and master a skateboard.

'You're still close, huh?' he asked, brow raised over tired eyes. 'Has he gone away to university?'

Lauren nodded, distracted by the sympathy in Mason's stare. She didn't want him seeing her so clearly, but his expression, his understanding seemed to open the floodgates on her confusion and doubt.

'I know it's silly,' she said, 'because he's only in Wellington, but I have to constantly fight the urge to call him, check he's okay, knows what brand of washing powder to buy,' she finished lamely. 'Turns out switching off the caring gene is tougher than I thought it would be.'

She should feel relieved that she'd finally have more time to focus on the promotion she craved now that Ben had left home. A few days ago, she'd even finally moved into the house she'd bought six months ago, which was within walking distance of the hospital.

'I'm sure you've helped to raise a fine young man,' said Mason, his deep voice inexplicably soothing, when with her behaviour so far and what she'd yet to tell him she hadn't earned his compassion. But he'd always been easy to talk to, one of the things she'd missed most about him when they'd split. That and the massive chunk of her heart he'd taken overseas with him.

'Try not to worry. He's probably having the time of his life.' He smiled, doing silly things to her insides. 'He'll be too busy to even care about laundry until his clothes start walking around on their own, or until he spots a girl he fancies and wants to make a good impression. Remember the state of my flat? Four boys sharing a house. Not much housework was done, I can tell you.'

That Mason remembered the bond she had with her brother made her take a fresh look at the man she'd been desperately trying to ignore since he'd walked back into her life. Of all people, Mason had been the one she'd confided in most about losing her mother and its impact on their family dynamics. How she'd lived at home as a student instead of sharing a flat with friends so she could assist her busy grieving father with childcare and school pick-ups, making dinner and homework supervision. She hadn't wanted Ben to miss out, and taking on some of her roles had allowed Lauren to feel close to her mother. Ben had deserved a supported childhood like the one she'd had. And, still grieving herself, Lauren had needed them as much as she'd figured they needed her.

Lauren took a deep breath, torn between holding back from him and laying all of her Ben-related concerns at Mason's feet. She blinked away the burn in her eyes. 'Trying not to worry about my baby brother is like herding cats. Impossible.'

'Well, he's not really a baby now, is he? He's only a year younger than I was when we first got together.' Something dark and seductive glowed in his eyes, like it had in her office yesterday, as if he was remembering again.

'I guess…' This conversation was going down a dead-end path. To steer herself away from that look and what it did to her skittish pulse, she blurted out a confession. 'I'm not sure I can take any credit for raising Ben. I didn't realise it at the time we broke up, but I still had a lot of grieving to do myself.'

He nodded as if he'd already figured that out, but also looked slightly taken aback at her overshare. 'Of course you did,' he said. 'You know, if you want to grab that coffee some time, we could talk properly. I'd love to hear what Ben is up to and how you've been.'

Lauren avoided his eye contact as she clawed her defences back into place. What was she thinking? No matter how tempting it was to confide in Mason, they couldn't be friends. She shouldn't even be talking to him.

'I'm sorry. That's not a good idea, I'm afraid.' She crossed her arms over her waist, guilt gnawing her stomach that she'd now need to backpedal.

When she met his stare again, she saw confusion and questions, felt their answering doubts tremble through her as the years slipped away. They could have been back on their beach, Lauren's bewilderment gripping her throat as she'd let him down as gently as possible and Mason simply walking away, no questions asked.

It was irrelevant after all these years, but

she couldn't seem to stop herself from dredging up the past, from saying, 'It wasn't an easy decision for me, you know, to change our plans and stay behind.'

He stared for long, intense seconds, during which Lauren squirmed and held her breath in foolish, misplaced anticipation.

'I never thought it was,' he said eventually, his eyes clouding over as if he was emotionally withdrawing.

He was right; there was no sense raking over ancient history. They'd each made their decision, gone their separate ways. Him being back now changed nothing. In fact, for her, it made everything way more complicated.

'Anyway—' she checked her phone for the time '—the reason I wanted to talk, aside from to apologise for yesterday, was to explain. There… um…there can't be anything between us now, other than a strictly professional relationship. Coffee dates included, I'm afraid.'

'Why? Just because we work together?' He frowned, his stare flicking over her features as if he considered arguing the point. As if he thought he could convince her, coax her out of herself, the way he had so many times in the past. 'I know we vetoed a wild sexual reunion when we spoke yesterday.' He offered her a playful smile she wanted to return. 'But it's not a crime for a couple of colleagues to spend time together away from work, especially when we used to be friends, didn't we?'

Lauren shrugged, bewildered and unable to concede a thing. They had been friends, but they'd been lovers first. Her body could recall the thrill of his every touch, her resolve tenuous as if being one sexy smile away from disintegration. She couldn't go there with him, of all people. Even a rekindled friendship could put her in an untenable position professionally. And she'd worked too hard.

'Friendship too is out of the question,' she said, her voice emerging unintentionally haughty, likely because part of her mind wanted to imagine exactly how that wild sexual reunion he'd mentioned might go. 'And please, let's try and keep this appropriately respectful.'

His eyes hardened, a frown forming between his eyebrows. 'I am trying, Dr Harvey. You're the one seeking me out in the car park. You're the one who led the conversation down a personal path.' He looked understandably upset.

'I'm not trying to imply that you've done anything wrong. This isn't personal.' She rushed to offer reassurance. 'But there can be no more talk of our past, or sex—' she held up her hand, cutting off his interruption '—no matter who starts it, and I'm aware that yesterday it was me.'

His jaw bunched, his defensive hackles rising. 'So this has nothing to do with distancing yourself from the infamous Murray Ward's son?'

Lauren gaped. 'Don't be ridiculous. I'm hurt that you would even think that of me.' She understood how he might be sensitive to any suggestion of frowned-upon conduct after his father's legacy. But his accusation made her feel as if he hadn't known her at all in the past, that she'd imagined their deep and passionate connection. Perhaps, desperate for solace in her grief, she'd invented his compassion when, in reality, maybe she'd actually meant nothing to him.

Well, she wouldn't fall into that same trap twice. She hardened her defences, rolled her shoulders back. 'This isn't about you. Mason. This is about my career.'

He frowned and Lauren pushed on. 'I'm one of the consultants on the appointment panel for the newest surgical consultant, the position I discovered yesterday that you've applied for.' She stepped closer, her determination rising. He needed to understand the predicament he'd inadvertently created for her with his return.

Why did he have to come back now, just when everything was finally falling into place for her? She was finally steering her own life on track after years of prioritising her family.

'I've spent years taking care of Ben and working my way up at GHH,' she said. 'I took the appointment committee position because I hope to secure a promotion as permanent Head of ER, a promotion I deserve.' Her eyes watered under his silent observation. 'I have your CV in my in-box, together with all of the other shortlisted candidates. It's a conflict of interest for me to associate with you in any way beyond professionally.'

Couldn't he see that?

'By acting professionally, I'm actually doing you a favour here,' she said, her resentment bubbling to the surface. In keeping Mason at arm's length, she was protecting not only her chances at the promotion she craved, but his too for the position *he* wanted.

'Doing me a favour? And what? I'm acting *un*professionally because I assumed that we could be friends?' Mason shook his head, his snort of incredulous laughter humourless. 'I understand what's going on now. This feels like déjà vu, after all.'

'What do you mean by that?' Lauren clenched her fists as if she could keep tight control of this slippery conversation.

He stepped closer, invaded her personal space so her body heated with more than indignation as his eyes sparked with defiance. 'Come on, Lauren, let's be honest. You've made difficult choices before, despite the way we once felt about each other.'

Lauren's jaw dropped but, before she could ask what his statement implied, he continued.

'Forget about it.' He placed the crash helmet on and tightened the strap under his chin. 'From now on I'll try to stay out of your way as much as is humanly possible. You won't have to compromise your promotion, not for me. We're both focused on career advancement. I just hope that you'll be able to appraise my CV with an unbiased eye, given that the respect and trust we once shared seems to be another casualty of the choices we've made. I hope your shift goes well, Dr Harvey.'

He'd respected and trusted her? He'd experienced conflicted feelings when she'd called it off? Shellshocked, Lauren watched him ride away, her heart in her throat, in no way mollified by their conversation. Her hope for a nice, tidy conclusion to the issue of him being back in her daily life drained away with the shudder of breath she exhaled. The only certainty to come from this interaction was that not only was Mason a constant reminder of what they'd once been to each other, he seemed to be suggesting there had been stronger feelings there on his side than she'd thought. With that in mind, the one thing she'd likely struggle to do was forget.

# CHAPTER FOUR

MASON MADE HIS way down the corridor towards the ER two days later, dread like ice in his veins. Despite what he'd promised Lauren when she'd practically accused him in the car park of acting unprofessionally on his first day at work, contact between them at the hospital was inevitable. Not that he could avoid her away from the hospital either. She filled his thoughts as he relived every word of their three incredibly frustrating conversations. Because he was clearly some sort of glutton for punishment where she was concerned, she even consumed his dreams—hot, sweaty, erotic re-enactments so far removed from the light flirtation she'd found so objectionable the other day he'd laugh if her rejection hadn't been so painful.

Lauren had always been a stickler for the rules, a planner, overthinking every possible eventuality in her mind until she'd figured out the best course of action. And, despite what she thought of him, he had no intention of making her professional life difficult. Of course she couldn't be seen to favour one candidate over another. Nor would he jeopardise his own ambitions, certainly not in *this* particular hospital, by fraternising with one of the appointment panel. Thanks to Murray, his own professional conduct had always been exemplary. He wanted to make a name for himself here, not give anyone an excuse to liken him to his father.

But with Lauren off-limits, even in the friendliest of ways, working at the same hospital could be potentially unbearable. No attraction, no intimate fantasies, no barely controllable temptation to touch her and see if it would feel as good as he remembered.

His pulse raced as he pushed into the department through the double swing doors, his body on high alert, his façade in place, ready to act as if they were complete strangers. The staff roster told him they'd be working the same shift, but so far he'd managed to go all day, almost to the end of the shift, without an interaction.

Resolved to avoid her as best he could, he entered the hectic resuscitation bay a nurse directed him to, braced for the urgent medical scenario beyond, but also braced for the sight of Lauren.

Of course she was there, supervising the controlled chaos of the emergency taking place.

Lauren glanced up as Mason hurried into the action. 'Dr Ward, thanks for coming,' she said, her voice tight, her exhale full of relief that went some way to soothing Mason's ego. Clinically, Lauren was more than capable of managing any case that came through the doors, but her reaction gave him a kick of satisfaction nonetheless. She needed him, if only in this moment of urgency.

'Dr Harvey, what do you need?' he asked, setting aside their personal issues and focusing on their young patient as he snapped on the pair of gloves he'd grabbed the minute he'd entered the bay.

So the sum of their relationship would be polite professional respect. He could live with that, even if the contrast between the expectations and possibilities he'd imagined and the reality left him unexpectedly empty.

Lauren beckoned him to occupy the other side of the stretcher as she listened to the chest of the young woman laid out there. Mason quickly introduced himself to the patient, who was conscious, her wide eyes full of fear, her spine immobilised by a hard collar and backboard, an oxygen mask covering her face and the various monitors reading her vital signs emitting their unique alarms in a jarring symphony.

Lauren tugged the earpieces of her stethoscope from her ears and gave him a succinct history.

'This is Cassie, a twenty-two-year-old, otherwise fit and healthy woman who fell from a second storey balcony. There's a flail chest and pneumothorax on the right. I've completed a bedside ultrasound and there's also a collection in the abdomen from a likely liver contusion, but we'll know more once we can stabilise her and get a CT scan.'

Mason nodded, his hands already completing his own examination of the woman's chest and abdomen, while he noted the patient's tachycardia and low oxygen saturation.

'I think she might be tensioning,' Lauren said as he took the stethoscope from his pocket. 'Grady is setting up the chest drain.' She glanced over her shoulder, where Grady was speedily preparing a sterile tray with the equipment they'd need to save Cassie's life.

When she looked back at him, their eyes met. Mason tried to convey calm assurance in his stare. 'Great. I'll take a quick listen of Cassie's chest.'

Despite their personal friction, they were competent medical professionals. They could handle anything together. Mason listened to Cassie's breath sounds, noting their absence on the right. He placed his fingers at the base of her throat, just above the suprasternal notch, and discovered that her trachea was deviated to the left.

'I agree with your diagnosis,' he said to Lauren, stepping away from the bedside for a few seconds to study the chest X-ray displayed on the overhead monitor, which indeed showed fractured ribs and a collapsed lung.

'Pneumothorax takes precedent over the abdominal injury,' he said, glancing expectantly at Lauren for her nod of assent.

'Agreed. Do you want to do it as you're here?' she asked, concern in her voice.

Like her, Mason was used to triaging patients with multiple serious injuries, albeit in field hospitals and the basements of bombed-out cities. If they didn't treat the tension pneumothorax, a life-threatening condition where air became trapped in the chest cavity with no escape, causing the lung to collapse and the heart and circulation to be compromised,

Cassie wouldn't live long enough to make it anywhere near an operating theatre.

'Any head injury, Dr Harvey?' asked Mason, quickly completing his own examination of the woman's rigid abdomen before stepping aside to wash up at the sink.

Lauren shook her head. 'But the neuro team are also on their way down. Spinal X-rays are also clear but we need to stabilise her in order to get her through to Radiology for a proper look.'

While Mason scrubbed at his hands and forearms, Lauren explained the procedure to the patient in a calm and clear manner.

'Dr Ward will be doing the chest drain,' Lauren stated to the gathered staff as Grady wheeled in the treatment trolley containing everything required to insert a chest drain into the patient's chest cavity to relieve the pressure on her lungs and, more importantly, her heart.

Mason dried his hands and put on sterile gloves.

'Has someone done a cross match for blood?' he asked, because if the chest drain didn't stabilise the patient's blood pressure he'd need to whisk her to Theatre to ensure she wasn't haemorrhaging into her abdominal cavity.

'Yes. Grady has organised all of the usual blood work,' Lauren said as she inserted another intravenous cannula into the woman's free arm. 'Anything extra you want while I'm here?'

'No, thank you.' Mason quickly cleaned the skin over the fifth intercostal space, injected local anaesthetic and made a small incision between the ribs. Lauren snapped on a pair of clean sterile gloves and joined him on his side of the stretcher, intuitively assisting him where needed, clamping the tube that would suck the air out of the patient's chest cavity with the proficiency of someone who, like him, had done this emergency lifesaving procedure a thousand times.

They moved in sync, anticipating each other's needs and moves as if they'd worked together for years, as if silently communicating their support and encouragement, all their personal distrust set aside.

The procedure necessitated their closeness. It was like a form of torture. He didn't want to notice the warmth of her body, hear the soft sigh of her breathing or be aware of her proximity with a strange intensity that he'd never experienced before, so he tried to block her out, focusing instead on the job.

No matter how well they'd known each

other six years ago, it hadn't been well enough. No matter how strong the physical attraction, it was irrelevant without trust. She'd stated what she thought of him, made her position clear once more, the same way she had when she'd ended things. Whatever they'd shared in the past, there was clearly nothing left as far as she was concerned.

He would master this physical attraction, ignore it until it passed. Hopefully one day he'd be able to see her around the hospital and not react at all beyond a polite smile of recognition.

Mason adjusted the position of the tube, his gloved hand colliding with Lauren's.

Inside he jumped as if he'd been zapped by an electric fence. He was so attuned to her proximity it was as if they'd touched for the very first time. Her muttered apology, the way she kept her gaze averted, only inflamed the tension.

How could he be so drawn to a woman who'd made it clear she wanted nothing to do with him? A woman who, even when they'd been in a relationship, had been emotionally withdrawn. Conscious of her grief and confused and uncertain of himself after the upheaval of his father's actions and mother's desertion, Mason had retreated too. When she'd broken things off with him without a backwards glance, he'd stuck to his plans and left everything behind when he'd left Auckland.

He hadn't seen it fully at the time, but they'd both chosen the easiest option back then, so it was clear to see now that Lauren was once more prioritising something over a relationship with him, even a friendship.

With steady hands he was acutely grateful for, Mason sutured the chest drain in place so it wouldn't fall out when the patient moved. Lauren unclamped the tube. Bubbles began to escape from the underwater seal immediately, telling them that the tube was correctly positioned and already allowing trapped air to escape. Within seconds, the patient's breathlessness eased, her colour improved and her heart rate approximated normal.

Mason caught Lauren's small sigh of relief. He glanced her way, nodded and, for the split second their stares locked, words passed between them once more. *Well done. We did it. Thanks for your help.*

He ached to be able to voice those things to her. But now he was too unsure of their forbidden situation to say any of that aloud. He didn't know how to act as if she meant nothing to him and refused to repeatedly humiliate himself.

They looked away in unison, the job coming before their personal issues as they continued their efforts to treat and stabilise the patient.

Mason placed his hand on Cassie's shoulder and smiled. 'Well done. That should make you feel a lot more comfortable. We're going to run a few more tests now, to have a look inside your abdomen, okay?'

They finished working on Cassie's care in silence, together but also apart. They'd never worked in the same department together before, training on different teams as medical students. And now, for the sake of their respective careers, they needed to maintain distance, pretend that there wasn't a connection between them, one that as far as Mason was concerned would not be silenced at present.

With the most life-threatening injury resolved, Lauren ordered a repeat chest X-ray and informed the orthopaedic surgeon and neurosurgical registrar of Cassie's status and other injuries. Mason passed on the patient's care to his on-call surgical colleague, happy that the patient's blood pressure and therefore the likely abdominal blood loss had stabilised. This would hopefully save her from an exploratory laparotomy, but with his shift over and other doctors already on the case he was now superfluous to requirements.

Heading out of the resuscitation bay, his feet dragged. He was physically tired, but for some reason the idea of going home to his empty house, alone, left him restless. Even the idea of a surf couldn't provide the usual uplift to his mood.

Hopefully it could be explained by the anticlimax, the plummeting adrenaline levels in his blood now that Cassie was stable. Or the impending funeral. It had been easy to shove his father's cremation from his mind while working, settling into a new department and establishing routines, but with free time on the horizon, free time in which thinking about Lauren was forbidden, his brain would ruminate, dissect his regrets in relation to Murray, ponder the overdue conversations for which it was now too late.

He swallowed the lump in his throat as he acknowledged the likely root of his reluctance to be alone with his thoughts. Lauren. Obviously he'd been more invested in seeing her, in starting up something with her than he'd recognised when he'd known he was returning home, because the hollowness inside him felt reminiscent of the grief he'd felt six years ago as he'd tried to put their relationship behind him and move on.

He spied her seated at the desk in the staff area, typing up her notes on the computer. His first instinct was to take the terminal next to hers to write up his own observations and the chest drain insertion procedure in the patient's hospital record before he left for the night. He could torture himself, prove that they could co-exist quite satisfactorily as colleagues, but he couldn't face the strained silence that would likely sour his day further.

Instead, he headed to the other staff area and took a seat next to Grady.

'Hey,' Grady said in welcome, his stare somewhat wary. 'Cassie has gone for a CT scan. Where's the boss?'

Mason logged into the computer system. 'She's still in Resus, doing what we're doing by the looks of it—writing up notes.' On the one hand he didn't want to talk about Lauren, but on the other she was pretty much his brain and his body's favourite subject at the moment, and Grady knew her better than anyone.

It was like a bad joke.

She was so close and yet a million miles out of reach. There might as well be a barbed wire fence around her adorned with a flashing neon *Entry Forbidden* sign.

'You all respect her a lot, don't you?' he asked.

Grady nodded. 'Her department runs like a well-oiled machine.'

'Unlike many I've worked in,' Mason agreed. In action, in calm, determined life-saving mode, Lauren was the sexiest thing he'd ever seen, not that he could admit that to her or to Grady.

The chasm between them emotionally plunged his mood into darker depths. Their former relationship had always been easy, intuitive, the way it had just been in the resus room when they'd worked side by side. There had been nothing they couldn't fix with a stimulating bicker, a joke around or a well-timed kiss. Until their very last issue, the one that had broken them apart: how neither of them had been ready to commit. How they'd dodged honesty and accepted the inevitable, dumping their relationship into the *too hard* basket and walking away.

Now, older and wiser, Mason would have handled things completely differently. But what about Lauren? Would she make the same choices today as she had then? She'd already admitted that she'd still been grieving for her mother. He'd felt let down by her at the time, but perhaps she'd felt nothing for him. She certainly seemed to be excelling at their current state of enforced avoidance.

She'd clearly done a better job of getting over their split than Mason.

'Is that why you came back? Because of the quality of our ER?' Grady was fishing, and Mason couldn't blame him. He was glad that Lauren had such a good friend in her camp.

'My father died,' he said without inflection. 'I came home to bury him, but it's good to be back at Gulf Harbour, to be honest. You know from your time in the army that there's no place like home.'

'I hadn't heard about your father. Sorry to hear that.' Grady fell silent in that way guys had of saying the bare minimum by stating all that needed to be said. The last thing Mason wanted to do was talk about his father.

'Does Lauren know?' Grady asked.

Mason clenched his jaw, shook his head, biting back the urge to admit that even friendship between him and Lauren was off the table. He'd never had the chance to tell her about Murray. Would she want to know?

Mason finished typing up his notes wordlessly and logged out of the hospital intranet. He and Lauren just weren't meant to be, not then and not now. If he'd developed the discipline to forgo creature comforts and work in some of the most basic places on the planet, surely he could harness the same discipline to forget about Lauren Harvey.

For the second time.

He stood, surprised to find Lauren staring at him from across the room. His pulse thrummed in his throat as he bid Grady goodbye and headed for the exit.

'Thanks for your help earlier, Dr Harvey,' he said as he passed, resigned to the fact that this cold tension would be their new reality.

'I…um… You're welcome, Dr Ward.'

There, he could do it, act unaffected. Only six years ago, the Lauren who was out of sight had been hard enough to forget. But seeing her again every day, unable to speak to her the way he wanted, to tease out her smile or seek out her company would test everything he'd believed about himself: that he'd be able to see her as a colleague and nothing else, that he didn't care what she thought of him, that he'd got over Lauren a long time ago. The truth was she could never be just another doctor, not to Mason. He knew intimate things about her body, her feelings, her dreams.

He exited the department without looking over his shoulder, even though the hairs on the back of his neck pricked up, urging him to look her way once more. But he didn't need to witness her indifference. Not again.

# CHAPTER FIVE

LAUREN SPRINTED DOWN the corridor towards the operating theatres, dodging porters wheeling patients on stretchers and in wheelchairs, ducking in between staff and relatives, her head about to explode with the urgency to catch up with Mason.

She rounded the corner, her heart thunking back into sinus rhythm as she spotted him just ahead. 'Mason, wait!' she called, relief a sweet taste in her mouth.

He spun to face her, the lines and angles of his handsome face wreathed in confusion, questions in his eyes. She stopped in front of him, catching her breath from both the sprint and his presence, close and tall, filling her vision, bathing her senses, corrupting her good intentions the way only a hot man or a slab of chocolate could.

She had no idea where to start; she only knew that, in light of what she'd just learned from Grady, she couldn't leave things with Mason the way they were.

Why hadn't he confided in her? She'd almost sobbed for Mason when she'd heard the news.

Glancing around the busy corridor, she moved to the wall, encouraging Mason to follow her so they'd be out of the stream of human traffic.

'Why didn't you tell me?' She moved closer and dropped her voice. 'About Murray?'

His eyes darkened, stormy and haunted. Before she was even aware of the comforting gesture, she gripped his arm. The warmth of his sun-kissed skin, the strength of the taut muscles beneath her hand and the flare of that familiar but also foreign heat in his stare, that even the way she'd hurt him the other day couldn't diminish, made Lauren drop her hand as if stung and shove it in the pocket of her white coat. 'I'm so sorry.'

For his loss, for the way she must have made him feel with her careless dismissal, and for touching him. Because not only was he regarding her from behind a detached and shuttered expression, something she deserved after she'd upset and insulted him, now her nervous system was lit up like a million stars, just the way it had been when they'd inadvertently touched in the ER while inserting that chest drain.

'Thanks,' he said, his jaw rigid. 'I'm sure that Murray would have valued your sympathy.'

The grim clench of his jaw called to Lauren. She wanted to be there for him the way she'd been when Murray had let Mason down so badly. And, irrationally, she wanted to kiss him, hold him, stay up all night talking to him.

How could she have convinced herself he'd be easy to ignore? How could she be so drawn to him after such a short time? How could all the emotions she'd bottled up after he'd left New Zealand still be there, pressure building, just waiting for something to pop the cork?

'I hadn't heard,' she said, recalling Mason's understandable confusion and anger when he'd learned of Murray's affair. Perhaps a part of him had never overcome the fallout—the break-up of his family. He would certainly have hated having to return to Gulf Harbour under such circumstances, to bury his father and not on his own terms.

'I wouldn't have expected you to have heard about it,' Mason said, crossing his arms over his chest, pain and rejection behind his words. 'It's not like anyone around here mentions Murray Ward's name. He's been persona non grata for years. They even renamed the Ward Wing.'

Lauren winced, because *that* she had known. The surgical wing of the hospital had been named after Mason's grandfather, Professor Isaac Ward, an eminent surgeon and researcher who had brought in millions of dollars' worth of funding over his years at Gulf Harbour. Mason had confided to her that he'd been particularly close to his grandfather growing up. With such a prestigious lineage, the Mason she'd first met had had big shoes to fill and for a while, before his father's fall from grace and the gossip that followed, he'd embraced the challenge, winning the Hiranga Cup for Excellence in his third year as a medical student.

Then, after his father had been forced to leave his head of surgery position after the extramarital affair with a much younger patient that had shocked the Gulf Harbour community, Mason had resented his father's hypocritical weakness, given his previous overbearing expectations. Unsurprisingly, Mason had grown more and more withdrawn and restless. Except the naive and emotionally fragile part of Lauren hadn't expected that withdrawal to extend to their relationship.

'Apparently,' he continued, a hint of bitterness in his voice, 'it was nothing personal, just part of a new hospital policy to create uniformity and inclusion. But Murray never quite overcame the slight. Not that he had any right to object, of course.'

'I'm sorry about that too.' Awash with so many conflicting regrets, Lauren looked down at her feet, wishing they were somewhere private. She had to fight the temptation to touch him again, to move closer to his warmth and strength and unique Mason scent. To offer him comfort he would probably reject, given the belligerent state of their current relationship.

But this was Mason, a man who'd been there for her, helped her through some of the darkest days of her life. Now that she knew the reason he'd returned, she wouldn't be able to stop thinking about him, grieving and alone. He carried the responsibility of being an only child and, despite his complex relationship with his father, Mason would always do the honourable thing.

'Grady told you, didn't he?' he asked, his stare roaming her features in a way that made her temperature spike uncomfortably.

'Yes,' she admitted, tentatively looking up at him from under her lashes, her gaze drawn to the set of his distracting mouth.

'But you could have told me yourself.' She tried to keep the hurt from her tone. After all, why would he have confided in her after her less than friendly reception, after she'd inadvertently all but accused him of acting unprofessionally? It seemed like a poor excuse now, but she'd been so rattled by his return, so desperate to do the right thing with regard to the appointment panel, she'd ended up being prickly and rude when he'd most needed a friend.

'Could I?' he said, his bold stare forcing her to admit her shortcomings where Mason was concerned. 'I'd planned to tell you, but we didn't stay friends when we broke up and you made it clear that we couldn't start again now.' He shrugged, his apparent nonchalance an irritating itch under her skin. She deserved some rebuke and she couldn't explain why it felt vital that he cared.

'When is the funeral?' she asked, ignoring his reminder of how cold she'd been. Now that she understood the circumstances, she was determined to be there for him, whether he wanted her or not. She too had known Murray Ward. Like most of the Gulf Harbour community, she'd respected him as a surgeon.

'It's Friday,' he said, his jaw tense, looking away over her shoulder.

She swallowed the swell of sympathy that rose up and inched closer into his personal space. 'Can you tell me what happened? How did he die?' Her voice was already a whisper, but the heat rising from his body seemed to steal her air.

Mason pressed his lips together, the emotions in his eyes conflicted, as she knew they would be. No matter how much he despised what Murray had done, no matter that his father had been cold and demanding, the man was someone Mason had once idolised, tried to emulate and impress.

'He collapsed on the golf course,' he said. 'A massive MI. Brought in dead at our neighbouring hospital.'

'I'm so sorry,' she said, her fingers desperate to reach for his hand. Her chest ached for him, for his broken relationships, his solitude. 'When did you last see him?'

When Mason had left Auckland, he and Murray had been practically estranged.

He pursed his lips as if debating how much to confide in her. She winced, recalling a time when the only people they'd been able to talk to were each other.

'I hadn't seen him in person for six years.'

'So you hadn't reconciled at all then?' Her throat clenched in sadness for Mason and

Murray's missed chances. Lauren had at least had time to say goodbye to her mother, not that it had made the grief any easier to bear.

Mason shook his head, his eyes turbulent with contained anguish.

Lauren's eyes stung with unshed tears. Despite holding such high expectations of his only son, Murray had let Mason down so badly through his actions, destroying his own career and their family in the process. Of course Mason had felt the need to get away from it all, to go and work where no one knew the Ward name. Seen in the rational light of time passed, she couldn't blame him. She hadn't blamed him at the time. She'd simply added more grief on top of her existing burden.

Lauren allowed her stare to hold his for long, intense seconds while her heart spasmed in empathy. She had to hope that she was conveying all of the things she was too scared to say, too scared to feel. A part of her knew this man better than she wanted to admit. She still needed to be careful around him for the sake of her equilibrium.

Mason stared back, the sincere non-verbal communication flooding every part of her body with awareness and impatience. Her jumbled thoughts turned selfish. Realistically, how long could Mason tolerate being in Auckland, with the bitter memories and constant reminders? Could Gulf Harbour ever fulfil him after living so long overseas? Would the lure of glory take him away again to a place where he could just be himself?

'Will Sarah be there on Friday?' Lauren asked to distract herself from how the idea of him leaving again racked her body with chills. She had no idea what kind of relationship Mason had with his mother now, but she remembered his devastation when Sarah had left for Australia after his parents' divorce. He'd felt abandoned, rejected, left alone to deal with the fallout of Murray's disgrace. Sarah had moved on, quickly remarrying and, it had seemed at the time, replacing Mason with her new stepson.

Oh, she'd invited Mason to go and live with her, but he'd still had two years left of his degree to finish. Unlike his parents, he wasn't free to up and leave all of the mess behind at that point.

'No,' he said. 'Her new husband has just had his first grandchild. She's moved on, and the last thing she'd want to do is be there for the ex who betrayed and humiliated her.' His voice was carefully devoid of accusation.

So he was truly alone.

Lauren's stomach pinched violently; she wished they were closer, physically and emotionally. But her conflict of interest wasn't the only reason she'd shunned his offer of friendship. Her physical reaction to him after all this time had terrified her. She needed to be vigilant around Mason Ward, to guard her soft spots more than ever.

'I'd have thought that she might want to be there for *you*,' she couldn't help commenting. After all, Sarah was his mother. She lived a three-hour flight away, and she only had one biological son. She didn't blame her for wanting a fresh start after her husband had cheated and created a scandal, but her rejection at the time had made things ten times worse for a confused and disillusioned Mason.

'I'm a big boy.' His voice was cool, his eyes hard, but sparks of determination and what looked like challenge sparked in their depths.

'Everyone needs someone for support.' He needed a friend and she could fill that role. She exhaled, feeling as if this older, more self-assured version of Mason was a total enigma after all. That shouldn't send flutters of excitement through her stomach, but it did.

'Can *I* come to the funeral?' she asked, desperate to ignore the way his proximity, the searching depth of his blue stare, made her feel edgy. 'I'd like to pay my respects. And I think someone should be there for you. Even an…old friend is better than nothing,' she added, stumbling over her words.

'I thought friendship between us was forbidden?' A hint of his mocking smile lifted one corner of his mouth, drawing Lauren's gaze back to his lips. Lips she'd worshipped, kissed a thousand times. Lips whose every uttered word she'd hung on.

'I thought you were accustomed to pushing the envelope?' she countered, because with him sparring came naturally.

He raised one eyebrow. 'I am. I was thinking more about you and *your* career, Laurie.'

Lauren steeled herself against the stupid warmth that spread through her veins at his words and the hint of tenderness that crept into his expression. How did he still know her so well?

She cleared her throat, resolved. 'It's a funeral for a doctor I knew who worked at this hospital. Let me worry about my career.'

Now would be the perfect time to tell him that she'd already spoken with Helen Bridges, Head of Corporate Management Services, and resigned her position on the interview panel. She'd hated to let down the other team members but she'd decided that, in view of her past with Mason, it had been the right thing to do.

Mason regarded her in silence for so long Lauren began to fidget, aware their interaction would appear intimate, aware of the sound of his breathing and the way his pupils dilated when he looked at her.

'Okay. Friends it is.' He nodded decisively, pushed his shoulder off the wall and began walking backwards away from Lauren so that their eye contact remained unbroken. There was no smile on his lips but Lauren could have sworn she spied a flash of triumph in his eyes.

How he managed the manoeuvre without bumping into anyone was quite a feat, but that was Mason. The laws of the universe didn't apply. After a few paces, he spun around and headed for the entrance to the suite of operating theatres.

Lauren stayed inert, her feet seemingly glued to the spot, trapped by the urge to watch him until he disappeared from sight. He swiped his security card over the scanner and pushed the door open and Lauren held her breath, the phrase *be careful* looping through her head.

At the last minute, Mason looked back at Lauren.

Caught staring, she gasped, gripping the handrail attached to the wall for support.

A sexy smile tugged at Mason's mouth. How had he known that she'd stood there watching him instead of returning to the ER?

Mason raised his hand in a salute and disappeared into the department, leaving Lauren bursting at the seams with her belly flutters and her scattered parts and a sense of inevitability that felt oh, so familiar.

# CHAPTER SIX

THE REMAINING FUNERAL GUESTS—a small handful of old university and golfing friends of Murray's and a couple of his distant cousins—still occupied one corner of the function room at the beachside restaurant where they'd gathered after the brief service at the crematorium.

With his duty as host largely over, Mason loosened and removed his black tie, folding it into his jacket pocket. He popped the top button on his shirt as he stepped out onto the deck into the sunshine in search of the one and only person he wanted to be around. Temporarily blinded by the bright sun, he dragged in the first deep breath of the day, relief erupting with his slow exhale as his gaze snagged on Lauren.

She hadn't left yet.

Mason paused, observing her where she sat on a low-slung bough of a pohutukawa tree that hugged the sand in a graceful and convenient arc. In a few weeks' time the entire tree, coined New Zealand's Christmas tree because it bloomed in December, would be dusted with its characteristic red flowers, providing a stunning photo opportunity.

Would they still be *friends* in December?

Would he ever be able to think of her in that way alone?

He shuddered, recalling how Lauren's presence throughout the sombre service that morning and the awkward social gathering that had followed had made the event tolerable. He'd felt strangely removed emotionally, as if he too was merely a funeral guest, his grief deficient from what it should be as Murray's son. Only the sight of Lauren's arrival, her taking a seat behind him as the service began—close enough to offer support, but not too close—had settled the sickening churning of his gut and brought him a sense of peace and homecoming for the first time since he'd set foot back in New Zealand.

Not that the serenity of her presence had lasted. How could it when their past and present were in such a convoluted mess?

Grateful that she'd insisted on attending, he headed Lauren's way, his mind replaying every frustrating detail of their conversations to date. The minute he stepped off the deck, his shoes sinking into the soft sand, he was on another beach at another time…

*'You've changed your mind?' he said, his voice incredulous from the sudden flare of nausea.*

*'Please try and understand,' Lauren pleaded, her eyes huge in the dusk light of their favourite beach.*

*Waves crashed behind them, seagulls screamed, their cries snatched away by the wind. Ice invaded Mason's bones.*

*'Ben needs me,' she said. 'He's only a little boy and Dad's still all over the place.' She looked down at her feet and Mason's stare followed, words deserting him. They'd planned this overseas trip for months, looked forward to it, saved up for the one-way air tickets to Europe. It was supposed to be their reward after graduation. Travel, working in foreign hospitals, adventure in far-flung places where they could be themselves.*

*Only Lauren already knew who she was. It was only Mason who needed to escape the Ward name, to go where no one knew the good and bad of his legacy.*

*'I can't leave.' Lauren's eyes filled with the sheen of tears. 'Mum would have wanted me*

*to be there for Ben, the way she was always there for us.' Her voice broke, her anguish crushing Mason's chest.*

*He tugged her into his arms, pressed his lips to the top of her head and sucked in the comforting scent of her hair. 'Of course he needs you. Don't worry, we'll figure it all out.'*

*He didn't have to know the right thing to say, he just needed to be there for Lauren.*

*A damp patch from her tears soaked through his T-shirt. He'd never seen her cry. They'd talked about her mother's death, about her concerns for her father, who'd started having some counselling. But Lauren had always held something back and, troubled by his own woes, he'd never pushed her too hard. That was why they worked so well; their relationship was easy, fun, and only heavy on the awesome chemistry.*

*Pulling back, Mason lifted her chin. He wiped her tears from her cheeks, kissing the wet paths they'd left behind, and then he pressed his mouth to hers. They'd sort out this blip together.*

*Lauren's lips were cold and tasted of salt. She sighed, her body shuddering as she collapsed her weight against him. Mason moved his mouth over hers in slow, soft seductive swipes. His blood heated, his body reacting as it always did to her closeness, but he kept the kiss PG, wanting to see her beautiful smile more than he wanted to drive them home as quickly as he could and distract her from her troubles in a different way.*

*'You should go to Europe anyway,' she said when he'd let her up for air, her stare serious.*

*His brain, still awash in a fog of arousal, scrambled to concentrate on what she was saying.*

*She tilted her chin in that determined way of hers. 'It's better for us both if we make a clean break of it now.'*

*'What?' His stomach started to fight its way into his chest, displacing his wildly panicked heart. He slid his hands from her shoulders and gripped both of her hands, certain that if he literally held onto her, her words would somehow make sense. 'Are you breaking up with me?'*

*This couldn't be happening.*

*She tugged her hands from his, wrapped her arms around her waist and turned away to face the sea. 'I have responsibilities here.'*

*How could her voice sound so cold? He wanted to block his ears.*

*'Neither of us went into this looking for anything long-term...' she shrugged, and Ma-*

*son's vision hazed out of focus '...and once we start work that will be all-consuming too...'*

*Mason cracked a little more inside; he was already bashed about by Murray's infamous affair, his parents' divorce and his mother's move to Australia. She might not have realised it—he hadn't himself until this very moment—but Lauren was all he had. Five minutes ago his exciting future had stretched ahead of him, one Lauren was part of. He'd leave Auckland, a place where, no matter what he did, he would always be compared to other Ward doctors. He'd been desperate to get away but hadn't once thought about ending things with Lauren.*

*'Wait...' He scrubbed his hand through his hair. Yes, they'd never talked about being together for ever or confessed deep feelings for each other, but she was just ending it like that, as if he'd meant so little to her all this time? 'Wait...' He didn't have to go to Europe. He paced, confused. Had he done something wrong? Been too wrapped up in his own issues to see her withdrawal? Perhaps she was telling him that she had no time for someone who'd been so tied up in knots over the mess his parents had created.*

*'It's for the best this way, Mason.' Lauren swallowed and he knew her mind was made*

*up. Once she made a decision, she stuck to it. 'I'm sorry that I'm pulling out, but you should still go.'*

*Mason choked on his disbelieving snort. She was breaking up with him and he could either stay and be alone, or leave and be alone.*

*Some choice she was giving him...*

'Hi. How are you doing?' Lauren's enquiry snapped him back into the present.

He blinked a few times, bringing the older Lauren into focus. 'I'll live,' he croaked, his throat dry from reliving her past rejection. 'I thought you might have left already.'

She stood from her perch on the tree, and he shoved his hands into his trouser pockets to stop himself from pushing back the lock of hair the light breeze had lifted onto her cheek. 'I wanted to talk to you before I go.'

Too restless to stand still, Mason slipped off his shoes and socks. 'Okay, in that case, let's go for a walk.'

'Are you sure?' Lauren frowned, her mouth pinched with worry. 'You're the host. You can't leave before all of the guests have departed.'

He shrugged, in no mood to make small talk. 'I can do what I want.'

If only that were wholly true where Lauren was concerned. They wouldn't be standing here if it were up to him. They'd be on his bike, heading somewhere neutral, somewhere lacking the power to trigger memories he'd rather forget, perhaps making new memories.

'I've done my duty as a son today,' he said. 'And I stopped caring what other people think of me a long time ago.'

Unlike the twenty-five-year-old who'd left New Zealand, the man she'd so easily thrown away, thirty-one-year-old Mason knew himself, understood his worth and his strengths and had his professional life, at least, all figured out.

His personal life still needed some work, though; something that had only become fully apparent when he'd reunited with Lauren.

'Come on.' He tilted his head in the direction of the shore and started walking.

He should tell her to go home. Her conflict of interest hadn't evaporated just because she'd learned about Murray's death. And the last time she'd been forced to make a choice he'd been the one to suffer the greatest consequences. He'd cancelled his ticket to Europe, packed up his ravaged heart and headed for the most inhospitable, isolated job he could find in Australia in an attempt to forget all about Lauren.

Too hot in the afternoon sun, Mason shrugged off his suit jacket, rolled up his shirt sleeves and returned his hands into his trouser pockets as he kept an easy pace, Lauren at his side.

'How are you really feeling?' she asked, her concerned tone brushing away the last lingering cobwebs of his bitter trip down memory lane.

He looked out to sea, focusing for a moment on his convoluted feelings about his father rather than his even more jumbled feelings for Lauren.

'I feel empty,' he admitted. 'Like I'm watching someone else's life unfold today, not my own.' Only now, with her walking next to him on the warm sand, doing something normal, something they'd done a hundred times before, did he feel like himself once more, not Murray's son, not Dr Ward, just Mason.

Of course he couldn't confess that, especially not to Lauren. It would cross some line he'd vowed to keep.

She nodded, empathy warming her stare. 'It's okay to have complex feelings today.

There are no rules when it comes to grief, as you know.'

Mason pressed his lips together. 'Complex sums it up perfectly,' he admitted, wishing, for some bizarre reason, he could reach out and hold her hand. For himself, for comfort. Platonic comfort... *Right.*

'I don't know... The service,' he said, 'it forced me to see my father's life as a whole, not just the mistakes he made in the latter years. He was difficult to please, had high expectations for his only son, but he was also a good father in other ways.'

He felt her hand on his bare arm and stopped walking, giving himself time to absorb the intimate heat of her touch. How could he switch off the physical craving, which seemed to only increase in intensity the more time they spent together?

She looked up at him, her eyes piercing him. 'I really do understand.'

'Of course. I know that you do.' He offered her a soft smile that he wanted to follow up by pulling her into his arms and tasting her lips. Instead he curled his fists inside his pockets.

'Thank you for letting me come today,' she said, her voice breathy with emotion in a way that made Mason want to glide his finger over those lips to see if they were as soft as he remembered. Except he'd all but rationalised that the best course of action was for him to make do with her offered friendship.

Instead he looked down to where her hand sat on his forearm. 'Aren't you worried about fraternising with one of the surgical consultant candidates?'

He wanted to rip out his own tongue, so tired was he of pretending he had no desire for this woman whatsoever. If she didn't care about crossing the line, why had he reminded her of it?

'I resigned,' she said, dropping her hand from his arm, crossing her arms over her waist and walking ahead once more.

*What? Had he heard her right?*

'From the appointment panel, you mean?' he asked, striding to catch up while his pulse tripped over itself to try and decipher her motivations.

She nodded, eyes front as if she didn't want to talk about it.

'I hope it wasn't because of me, because you were right. You do deserve that promotion.'

She shot him a sideways glance, her expression unreadable. 'I did it for me. I discussed it through with Corporate Management Services and I decided that our…past relationship was enough to create a professional conflict. If I'm the best candidate for the Head of ER position, it won't matter that I've pulled out of a commitment I'd struggle to handle objectively.' She looked down, kicked at an oyster shell with her toe. 'At least I hope it won't.' She gave a humourless snort and the spaghetti in Mason's head twisted a little more. If he'd thought he hadn't known where he was with the Lauren of six years ago, today's Lauren could tie him into even tighter knots. He'd need to beware, keep his guard up, lock away his feelings.

Then it suddenly occurred to him, as if he'd just dived under the waves out in the bay, the cold shock slapping him to his senses. The ethical barrier to their friendship was gone, like a puff of smoke.

He should feel relief. Excitement was there, but that was pretty constant in Lauren's presence, given their chemistry. But the overriding emotion in him was confusion. Her resignation changed nothing. Only she'd been concerned enough about her past feelings for him to pull out of the interview process.

Did that mean she'd had stronger feelings back then than he'd known about at the time?

He mentally slapped himself. Today was

not the day to try and come to important conclusions.

'I haven't said it yet,' he added, 'but I really appreciate you being here today.' He cleared his throat, embracing the vulnerable feeling that he couldn't seem to shake every time they talked.

She frowned, looked down as if ashamed. 'Even though I inadvertently insulted you and rejected your offer of friendship because I was being a bit uptight about my job?' She gnawed at her lip as she waited for his answer, but there was that hint of a smile in her eyes, a flash of the old Lauren, the one who could give as much as she got when it came to teasing and bickering and goading each other on.

Mason grinned, nodded. 'Even then.' Falling serious, he added, 'Today would have been intolerable without you. Thank you for coming.'

'You're welcome.' Her expression softened, her eyes dancing over his features in the way that told him she had a hundred thoughts in her head. He wished he knew what they were.

'You know, my experiences with Ben have taught me that parenting sometimes feels like an impossible task. Your father was a very intelligent man. I bet he hated knowing he'd let you down by his actions.'

Mason swallowed, torn between keeping things superficial in order to keep her literally at arm's length and confiding his deeper feelings and inadequacies to the only woman he'd ever allowed close, not that it had saved him from pain. Her protective, nurturing role with Ben gave her a mature understanding of relationships, and talking about his father would stop him trying to dissect their current bewildering situation.

He exhaled, content for now to have her friendship. 'I used to feel so angry that he'd abused his position of power. And then I'd feel guilty for judging my own father, a brilliant and diligent surgeon, a man who had done so much good before making one bad choice.'

She nodded in understanding, stepping closer to his side. 'I used to be angry that my mother had left us, even though the rational part of me knew she'd had no choice. Emotions aren't always logical,' she said gently.

'I could have forgiven him,' he carried on, 'if he hadn't continued to be the sanctimonious tyrant he'd always been. Perhaps then his actions wouldn't have been so utterly hypocritical. I grew up hearing how he was continuing my grandfather's legacy, building on the Ward name, but when I said I wanted to follow in both their sets of footsteps and study medicine it seemed that nothing I ever did was good enough. And yet he was the one to throw it all away. He was the one to let himself and others down.'

'It's hard when you realise a man you'd once looked up to is fallible. Flawed.' She shrugged, looked out to sea. 'But we're all human. We all make mistakes.'

She fell quiet, as if putting distance between him and the emotional vulnerability of her confession. Mason wanted to ask if he featured in her regrets, but he didn't want anything to damage their newly found friendship. Instead he said, 'Today must have been difficult for you too. Brought up painful memories of your loss.'

'I'm fine. I've had longer to come to terms with my grief, and at least I got to say goodbye to Mum.' She smiled in reassurance. 'I'm sorry that you didn't have that opportunity with Murray.'

As if in silent agreement, they turned and headed back the way they'd come. Neither spoke, the quiet companionable, so that Mason wondered if perhaps this friendship thing might work.

After a while, Lauren looked him up and down. 'You know, you're different now. You've changed in a positive way. You never used to admit to having any weaknesses or regrets.'

'Maybe that's what age does,' he replied with a smile. 'And you've changed for the better too. You have less barbed wire around you than you used to have.' Not that being close to her wasn't still dangerous.

When they reached the car park next to the restaurant, Lauren dropped her shoes and slipped her feet inside.

'Want a ride home?' Mason did the same and then made his way to his bike and unlocked his helmet. 'I always carry a spare.' He knew she'd arrived by taxi.

She looked at his bike as if it were a double bed, all of her former wariness returning. 'I'm okay, thanks. Look, I don't want to give you the wrong idea. I do want us to be friends, but I'm not looking for a relationship. My priority is still my promotion—'

'And mine is the surgical consultant job,' he interrupted, because they'd covered this ground before and he didn't need a replay of how anything beyond friends was of no interest to her. There were only so many rejections a man could take. 'So, neither of us is in a relationship kind of place.'

She nodded as if appeased; only a small frown pinched her lips. 'Good. That's cleared that up then. Are you going to Grady's birthday drinks tomorrow? He took a lot of persuading that he should mark the occasion for once. Molly, his daughter, is with his ex for the night, so he'll need us to help distract him.'

'In that case, I wouldn't miss it,' Mason said, happy to be included in the invitation.

'It's at the Har-Bar. Seven p.m.' The mention of the bar they'd frequented, playing out much of their former relationship—dates, celebrations, fights and making up—forced a boulder of trepidation into Mason's gut.

'Great,' he said, ignoring the hesitant way Lauren was looking for his reaction. 'I'll see you there.' He jammed on his crash helmet and revved the engine of his bike, climbing aboard and heading for the road. He could do this, keep her at arm's length, be her colleague and her friend.

He could do it, but it would test every atom of his being.

# CHAPTER SEVEN

LAUREN GLANCED AT the door of the Har-Bar, her teeth nibbling at her bottom lip and her nerves jangling with anticipation. Most of the invited guests were already gathered to celebrate Grady's birthday. The bar was packed, the atmosphere buzzing and Lauren couldn't seem to enjoy herself at all.

Grady thrust a glass of wine into her hand and she muttered her thanks.

'Why don't you text him if you're going to watch the door every five seconds?' her friend asked, a small frown tugging at his mouth.

'Text who?' Lauren replied, turning her back to the door and plastering an *I'm having a good time* smile onto her face.

'Mason,' Grady said, smiling a greeting to someone in the far corner of the bar before shooting Lauren a reproachful stare.

'Why would I be waiting for Mason? It's

*your* birthday.' Why couldn't she stop thinking about Mason? It was as if since the funeral he'd infected her mind, multiplying exponentially there like a virus.

'Because you've been different since he arrived back,' Grady said in his no-nonsense way. 'I wondered if some of the old feelings have resurfaced.' The sympathy in his voice grated against Lauren's eardrums. Was she that obvious? Had she been moping around the hospital, pining for a glimpse of Mason like a lovesick puppy? She shuddered at the thought.

'Don't be ridiculous. How have I been different?' She took a massive gulp of wine to ease the feeling that she was spinning out of control and everyone was watching.

'Distracted. A bit up and down. I think the new registrar thinks you hate her,' he said, glancing over at Kat Collins, the newest doctor to join Gulf Harbour ER.

Kat paused in her conversation and smiled hesitantly at Lauren and Grady from the other side of the bar. Aware that the younger woman might, quite rightly, assume that they were talking about her, Lauren beamed her friendliest smile.

'She does not,' Lauren hissed at Grady when Kat continued her conversation.

Grady shrugged. 'No, you're probably right. I hardly know her. So,' he said, changing the subject, '*are* you and Mason seeing each other again?'

Lauren sighed; Grady could be like a dog with a bone sometimes. 'Of course not.'

'Nothing going on at all?' Grady pressed.

'We're colleagues and friends. That's it.' Only ever since he'd confided in her about his relationship with Murray, Lauren couldn't help feeling closer to him, and that was without the incendiary attraction she needed to constantly tame with a combination of denial, avoidance and stern self-talk.

The more she saw of him, the hotter he seemed to become. Perhaps because he was so much more self-assured than younger Mason had been, more confident in his own abilities and unconcerned by trivialities. Or perhaps it was because he was respecting their new friendship, following her rules, no more of the flirtation he'd tried on when he'd first returned. No, that couldn't be the reason she wanted to rip his clothes off every time she saw him at the hospital because, truth be told, his cool, collected consideration was driving her crazy with need.

'No. No way, nuh-uh,' she emphasised.

'We've been there, done that. I won't be making the same mistake twice.'

Grady shifted and she flushed, aware that she'd voiced her utter determination not to mistake great sex for a relationship aloud. Not that she wanted a relationship.

She looked up to see his worried expression. 'That's quite a protest.'

'Well, stop asking silly questions then. The only thing causing my distraction, if I have been distracted, is Ben. I'm worried about him. He hasn't called either me or Dad for over a week.'

'He's too busy having a good time.' Grady grinned. 'Surely you remember what it was like to be a student.'

She did, especially once she and Mason had become an item. And she was back to thinking about him again.

'It's okay,' Grady said. 'Completely letting go of an ex is hard, especially when they are part of your daily life, whether you want them to be or not.'

Lauren tilted her head and offered her friend a sympathetic smile. Carol, Molly's mother dipped in and out of their lives when it suited her, leaving Gardy to comfort their daughter when she left, even though they'd been divorced for years and were supposed to have a specific shared custody agreement.

'You're right,' Lauren said. 'It has been hard seeing Mason every day, especially in the beginning. But we've put the past behind us and moved on as friends. I promise I'm not going to allow myself to get hurt again.' She rested her hand on Grady's forearm to reassure him. 'It took me years to get over him the first time around. I'm not stupid. Now. Can we please talk about something else?'

To her surprise, Grady's complexion turned a little grey. 'I thought you got over him after that first month. That's what you told me.'

Lauren sighed. 'Eighteen months, one month, what's the difference?'

'Quite a big difference, actually.' He dropped his head back and gazed up at the ceiling as if seeking patience from the heavens.

'Don't get your undies in a twist,' Lauren snapped. 'It was my broken heart, not yours.'

When he settled his eyes on her once more, his serious expression gave her chills. 'He called, Lauren, about eight months after he'd left.'

Lauren's stomach twisted with dread. 'What? Called who? What are you talking about?'

'Mason—he called the ER to talk to you. It was the night you'd gone out with Greg, that army buddy of mine, remember? I finally talked you into your first date since you'd split up with Mason.'

Lauren nodded, her head spinning at his bombshell. She'd had a couple of drinks with Greg, which had been enough for her to determine that she wasn't ready, that all she could think about was how Greg wasn't Mason, how it hadn't felt right.

'Why didn't you tell me?' she whispered, the hand holding her wine glass trembling. What did it mean? What had Mason wanted? Had he called to catch up on the hospital news, or had he called for her, because he hadn't been able to move on either?

Grady winced, shamefaced. 'I wanted to tell you but he asked how you were, and when I told him that you were out on a date he made me swear, man to man, that I wouldn't tell you. He didn't want it to upset you. He said he wasn't ready to come back to New Zealand anyway and he was happy that you were moving on with your life.'

'Grady,' Lauren groaned. She placed her glass on the bar and clutched her hand to her churning stomach. It shouldn't matter. It was in the past. She thought back to that time.

She'd just started her registrar job in Emergency Medicine. The hours were long, the stress levels insane. Ben was fifteen and in the full throes of his first teenage rebellion. Their father and he had butted horns regularly and Lauren had somehow ended up with the role of peacekeeper.

It had been a mess. No wonder her first foray into dating after Mason had been a disaster. She hadn't been ready.

But she had moved on eventually and if she'd known about his call at the time it would have changed nothing. She had still been tied to Auckland, and Mason had clearly been happy overseas.

Except she'd never know what it might have meant at the time, and she couldn't for the life of her decipher if it made any difference now. Had Mason had regrets? She'd always assumed that he'd moved on without a backwards glance six years ago, her conscience clear because she might have been the one to call it off in her sensible, rational way, but he hadn't argued or kept in touch.

But now she knew differently…

With exquisite timing, Mason chose that precise moment to arrive. Lauren was so confused she could barely look at him as he greeted Grady and wished him a happy birthday.

She could smell him though, his sexy spicy aftershave making her dizzy.

Mason handed Grady a small wrapped gift. 'It's an African fertility statue. It represents health, wealth and personal happiness.'

Grady laughed and unwrapped the gift while Lauren sneaked a glance at Mason. He wore a dark T-shirt and black jeans, which were loose and comfortable-looking but hugged all the defined parts of his body like a lover's caress. She wanted to throttle him for the promise he'd extracted from Grady five years ago, then she'd throttle Grady for being stupid enough to keep secrets from her, and if he'd survived the first attack she'd throttle Mason again. Either that or she'd kiss the life out of him until she understood her erratic emotions.

Finally, she met his eyes, a fizzle of arousal spreading along her nerves as she swam in their striking blue depths. He smiled, friendly enough, only with Grady's news colouring everything she thought she knew about the past she searched his stare for answers, an explanation, something, anything to steer her back to a sure footing.

'This place hasn't changed at all,' he said as

Grady became swept away into another conversation with his fellow ER nurses.

'The menu has improved,' she said, trying and failing to block out the rush of memories of them here together, a movie-style montage of many of their most memorable moments: the exact table where they'd had their first date, the corner where they'd hissed their first fight, the alcove near the bar where they'd kissed and made up because neither of them had been able to stay angry with the other for long.

'How was your day?' he asked.

'Good. Yours?' Tension pounded at her temples. She wanted to drag him into a quiet corner and demand an explanation. 'Aren't you going to get a drink?' she said before he could reply.

He studied her for a few seconds. 'In a moment. Are you okay?'

No, she wasn't. Everything was shifting under her feet. She didn't know this man; perhaps she'd never fully known him.

'Lauren…?'

She glanced around the bar for a discreet nook where they could talk in private, but the place was packed. Instead, she leaned close, raising her voice over the din.

'What did you mean the other day when

you said we'd made a difficult choice, despite the way we once felt about each other?'

Mason frowned. 'Why are you bringing that up? I thought we'd decided on friendship.'

She should let it go and do exactly that, except she'd always assumed that Mason had walked away from their relationship unscathed. That they'd come to an inevitable conclusion after graduation. That he hadn't been ready for commitment anyway and her decision to stay behind had merely brought their split forward by a few months.

Lauren raised her mouth to his ear. 'Grady just told me about you calling the ward to speak to me eight months after you left.' Warmth emanated from his body, the clean spicy scent of him making her legs a little unsteady.

She pulled back and stared, every beat of her heart palpable. He watched her for a few beats and Lauren's patience snapped. 'Why, Mason?'

He sighed, glanced away and then met her stare once more with a shrug. 'I wanted to know you were okay.'

'But why?' This close to him, his eyes deep emotive pools, her confusion amplified. Had there been more than concern? Had he struggled to forget her? Could it be that they'd both had stronger feelings than they'd let on at the time?

'I don't know, Lauren.' He pressed closer so her breasts were only an inch from his chest, blue flames flashing in his irises. 'Maybe because I was homesick. Maybe because I'm a nice guy who cared about you.' He glanced at her mouth and then made eye contact again. 'Maybe because you pushed me away and I hadn't been ready to let you go yet. I missed you, fool that I was.'

She gasped, her pulse raging in her ears. She'd known that she'd let him down, that he'd been disappointed. But she'd understood that he'd needed to leave and she hadn't wanted to hold him back. She hadn't fully realised how she'd felt about *him* until it was too late and he'd left the country, until she was once more abandoned and hating the concept of any emotion that had such power to make her feel as if she had a limb missing.

So she'd blocked her heartache out of her mind, the way she'd blocked out her mother's death. But of course she'd missed him too. She'd grieved for him. She'd assumed a clean break was for the best, but a part of her had wanted, hoped that he'd call or email or come home. She'd almost contacted him a hundred times.

Lauren sighed, emotionally drained.

'Why does it matter now?' Mason asked, his stare tracing her features, landing on her mouth and then returning to search her eyes. She had no answer. Tingles buzzed over Lauren's skin. The bar was too loud. Too warm. She couldn't breathe.

'I need some air,' she said, her hand clutching her throat.

Concern replaced the intensity of his expression. 'Let's go outside.' He took her elbow and steered her to the door, weaving them between the full tables. They bypassed the handful of occupied outdoor tables underneath brightly coloured umbrellas. It wasn't until they made it to the pavement just outside the closed tattoo parlour next door that she managed to take a full breath.

'Do you need to sit down?' he said.

She looked up from where she'd been bent double, hands braced on her thighs. He appeared lost, uncomfortable, his hands shoved into the pockets of his jeans, out of the way.

There was no way she could fall apart while he remained coolly detached. She straightened, dragged in a restorative breath. 'I'm fine. I'm just trying to make sense of what happened between us six years ago.'

Lauren forced herself to examine those last

few weeks of their relationship. At the time, she'd felt as if they'd both played a part in their demise.

The changes in Mason the minute his world had imploded when his father's scandal became known and his mother left the family and New Zealand behind had initially been understandable and she'd done her best to support him through those tough times. He'd grown more and more restless, desperate to graduate, desperate to get out of there, and Lauren had been forced to take a reality check, to question everything and to finally admit that the writing was on the wall.

'I was a bit all over the place,' she added when he stayed silent and watchful. 'Trying to do the right thing by my mother, who I still missed so much I doubted every decision I made, and by Dad and Ben.'

He'd been going to leave, no matter what, and still confused by divided loyalties, with the depth of her feelings that she just hadn't been in a position to trust and scared that she'd be hurt, Lauren had retreated behind her own defences.

They were so different. They'd never once confessed that they were in love or even serious about one another. Their priorities beyond their careers felt at complete odds. Of course she'd had to look to the future and make a choice. And so had he.

She'd pushed him away before she'd been pushed away by him, protecting herself from heartache.

And now what? Did the fact that he'd called her all that time ago mean that the blame for their split lay solely at her door after all...?

He pressed his lips together in a grim line. 'I know all about your responsibilities. I respected your decision, didn't I? I did exactly what you told me to do.'

'But I let you down?' Lauren asked, because she could see the ghost of his hurt in his stare.

He clenched his jaw, clearly not about to admit a vulnerability. 'Why are you raking over this? I'm trying my best here.' He scrubbed his hand through his hair and turned away. 'Just let it go, Laurie.'

Laughter boomed from a group seated outside the Har-Bar. Mason paced further out of earshot, loitered under the awning of the neighbouring estate agent. Lauren's temperature rose as she strode after him. She touched his arm and he spun to face her.

'Hold on a minute. What are you trying your best to do?' she asked.

His eyes blazed with fire. He dropped his gaze to where her hand still sat on his arm.

She snatched it away. She didn't want to lead him on, but something in her couldn't allow them to wriggle out of this confrontation. She'd resigned from the appointment panel in order to do the right thing. The least he could do was explain himself.

'I'm trying to be your friend, as requested,' he said.

Lauren huffed, indignant. 'Well, don't do me any favours. You're free to abandon this friendship if it doesn't work for you.' Needing to get away from the way he was messing with her resolve, Lauren marched around the corner of the building.

Growing aware of her surroundings, she recognised the familiar alleyway that ran behind the block of eclectic shops surrounding the Har-Bar, which was another part of their history. They'd made out in it too many times to count, too horny to wait until they reached home. They'd even had sex here once, hidden by the shadows of the early morning hours and the neighbouring buildings.

The hairs on the back of her neck prickled and she sensed that Mason had followed her into the alley. She faced him, trying to ignore the way her body incinerated at the sensual memories of this place.

'And how is our friendship working out for *you*?' Mason stepped closer so Lauren had to tilt her chin to keep eye contact. 'Why are you so upset to learn that I still cared about you long after you pushed me away? Long after you yourself had moved on?'

'I didn't have to push that hard, did I?' Her heart pounded so fast she took a step back. 'You agreed to leave pretty readily. So what are you trying to say? That you actually had strong feelings for me or something?'

She laughed, actually laughed, because the idea was so preposterous. She hoped that only she could hear the nervous echo to that laughter. Hoped he couldn't see the excited pulse throbbing in her throat because he was so close she could see flecks of silver in his irises, feel his breath on her lips, almost taste the intoxicating flavour of him.

Their staring match seemed to last an age, neither of them willing to concede defeat. Why could he still get to her this way? She was older, supposedly wiser, more experienced and the stakes were higher. And yet he still had the power to make her feel reckless and unstable, as if she'd do anything for him.

'I'm saying,' he replied after so long that

Lauren thought the lust boiling in her veins might have made her deaf, 'that you're the closest I've ever come to a relationship and the only favour I'm doing you is to pretend that we aren't still insanely hot for each other.'

Stunned, she scraped her eyes over his features, willing him to be as conflicted as she felt. She was more than hot; she was incandescent for him. But how dare he throw down some sort of sexual gauntlet? She had been doing just fine since his return, all things considered. Sure, she either hid in her office to avoid him or watched the door of the ER like a possessed fan stalking a celebrity for a glimpse of his confident swagger, but that was just to ensure that she appeared professional. He was her ex after all.

But they weren't at work now. And all she could think about was how good it would feel to admit he was right, to kiss him and finally dispense with all of this distracting sexual tension.

'You are so infuriating,' she said through gritted teeth, trying not to think about sex—sex with Mason and just how good it had been. Yes, their chemistry was as intense as ever, but unlike when they were younger and their differences had driven her so crazy that she'd had to kiss him instead of throttle him,

Lauren was now more in control of her emotions, and her urges, and if at thirty-one she was his only relationship, he was clearly as commitment-shy as ever.

A hint of an indulgent smile twitched on his lips, drawing her eyes there. She took a step back towards the wall of the alley.

'And you still overthink everything,' he said, following, step for step, as if they were snarled together in the same net, entangled and helpless and unable to get away from each other.

Surely he couldn't like her worst personality trait—endless future-gazing, the mind-draining consideration of the pitfalls of each and every decision.

'Do you remember this place?' he asked, one eyebrow raised in challenge as if she'd deliberately chosen that location for this conversation.

Her body shuddered, liquid heat in every blood vessel as their eyes remained locked. He was right. The passion still flared between them and she'd been a fool to think she could just deny it and carry on as if he was any other doctor. He knew it, Auckland knew it, this very alleyway knew it, mocking her.

'Of course.' Her voice was a needy whisper that made her cheeks flush. She was practically inviting him to re-enact those erotic scenes she couldn't seem to scrub from her mind.

Torn to the point of utter desperation, Lauren reached out, grabbed at the hem of his T-shirt, not tugging nor releasing her grasp. Her gesture confirmed what her eyes and her inertia and her lack of denial blasted. She was too scared to say the words, but powerless to stop her actions.

How could she want him so much? Beyond reason and sense and consequence.

Her breaths had become shallow, rapid. One kiss would likely be enough to destroy all of the memories of how good it had been before, because surely she was inflating the truth? Then they could resume their working relationship as if it had never happened.

Lauren's back hit the rough stone wall of the building they'd just left, the air knocked from her lungs in a soft gust of release as Mason closed the distance.

Still gripping his shirt, she abandoned the fight, all rational arguments dissolving in the face of the familiar heat in his eyes and how it seemed to inflame her further until she was burning up.

Slowly Mason braced one hand on the wall beside her head and raised his other hand, his fingertips tracing the curve of her cheekbone and the angle of her jaw, the way he used to when they lay facing each other in bed. He'd once said that he'd never seen anything as perfect as her, that he couldn't believe that she'd chosen him, and then he'd spoiled it, laughed at himself and apologised for being 'soppy'. She'd considered it his most vulnerable moment until he'd talked about his father after the funeral and she'd witnessed all the parts of himself he'd hidden as a younger man.

Mesmerised by his touch, because it felt new, different, enthralling in a way she couldn't untangle, she pressed her cheek against his palm. Perhaps because he was silently staring, no humorous observations to ease the building tension, as if waiting for her permission.

This was so stupid. Just because she knew something would feel so good didn't mean she should do it. But her body seemed to have disconnected from her brain, clearly intent on making its own reckless decisions.

'What are we doing?' she asked on a breathless whisper that sounded worryingly needy as she gripped his T-shirt tighter, pulled him closer.

What was *she* doing? more importantly.

She should withdraw from the intense and purposeful look in his eyes, push him away emotionally even if she lacked the strength to do it physically, make some joke as he had back then.

His eyes shone with risk, danger, exhilaration, all the things he represented to Lauren. 'I'm showing you why us being just friends is a pipe dream.' Mason inched closer so that only a few centimetres of space separated their bodies. Lauren looked down and spied the reason; somehow she'd subconsciously hooked her fingers into the belt loops on his jeans the way she'd used to.

The air buzzed with static as Lauren tried to formulate some witty one-liner to remind him that she was a mature woman in charge of her emotions and her hormones, only her body betrayed her. She raised her hands, desperate for the strength to push him away so she could escape the feral look in his eyes, one she'd never seen before. Instead her fingers curled into his shirt over his chest.

It was simply chemistry, its power likely halved the minute they both acknowledged it and then moved on. It would only be one kiss. She could stay detached.

Mason groaned at her touch, his eyelids drooping with arousal, his leg slipping between hers, his thick hard thigh just there, a perfect height for riding.

Still he denied her his mouth, which hovered a hair's breadth from hers. Was this her punishment for throwing up barriers? Would she need to beg? And how did he know she was so close to doing exactly that?

'Laurie…?' His breath gusted over her lips where she'd unconsciously wet them with her tongue. His eyes, which carried the same question as he'd injected into her whispered name, bored into hers so deeply she feared that he'd see her every buried secret thought, see how much she wanted him, how much he'd upended her calm, orderly and responsible life with his return. How the professional grown woman and responsible doctor wanted to lose herself in passion for a second until her mind cleared of the past, where she'd clearly built Mason up to fantastical proportions, and forgot her worries for the future.

Resigned, she couldn't deny herself just one familiar kiss. She raised her chin, tugged at the fistfuls of his shirt and dragged his mouth the final space to hers, her body acting on instinct and her brain turning to mush.

*Nothing* about the kiss that followed was familiar.

As if he needed her to breathe, Mason engulfed her entire being, his hard body pressing her into the wall as their lips met, their mouths consumed.

Lauren moaned, parting her lips, seeking his tongue, diving right back into their former level of intimacy as if they'd never stopped doing this, as if the intervening years—years of loneliness and doubt—had never happened.

Had their connection ever been this passionate? This honest and desperate, as if neither of them could get enough of the other, as if they'd denied themselves for too long and by tasting each other, swallowing up every moan and sigh and grunt, somehow made up for every day of the past six years apart.

Lauren grew dizzy, desperate to take a huge gulp of air, but instead she tangled her fingers in his hair to hold his mouth close, scared to break the bond, scared to come to her senses. She didn't want this one kiss to be over.

Mason's hands gripped her waist, the bump and grind of their hips turning X-rated to any passing observer. But Lauren couldn't find the strength to care. He'd reduced her to a woman willing to take risks, to act like a teenager, snogging in public. She clung to the selfishness of her actions, dragging every scrap of pleasure from her recklessness, soared, free for the first time in years of the compulsion to put other's needs above her own.

But her over-analytical mind refused to wallow in pleasure alone. What if she'd never pushed him away six years ago? What if they'd parted for no reason?

It struck her with the force of a blow to the ribs. No matter how much she'd denied it at the time, how often she'd refused to contemplate the truth after he'd left when the pain finally struck, a part of her had had deep, deep feelings for him back then and she'd been terrified of what might happen. Of what had, in fact, happened. That she'd make herself that vulnerable to another person and he'd leave her anyway.

But this stolen moment of lust had nothing to do with feelings. She'd made her choices. She'd sacrificed him and any other relationship to focus on family and work, all she could fit into her life. And she would sacrifice this undeniable connection to him yet again for her career and her ongoing peace of mind.

She broke free, tearing her mouth from his. 'This is a bad idea.'

Like the first chunk of chocolate from the bar, his kiss was too good, too addictive, too rewarding, lighting up her brain's poor starved pleasure centres like the fireworks over the Harbour Bridge on New Year's Eve. She couldn't garner the strength to make it stop completely, dragging him back for another kiss, another moment of reckless pleasure.

'I know, I know,' he mumbled against her lips, kissing her again with similar desperation, his hands cupping her face, his fingers tunnelling into her hair as he slanted his mouth over hers and led them both back into irresistible abandon.

For a split second she imagined him inviting her back to his place, heard herself accepting, envisioned them naked and tangled up in sheets, her body fully on board with the fantasy.

Dragged into reality by her keen readiness to take this further than a kiss, Lauren's blood ran cold. He'd been back for five minutes and she was already forgetting about everything else and acting recklessly with Mason in a dark alley. A kiss she could rationalise, mitigate, but living out the fantasy, sleeping with him, would be no casual thing, not now. And, as Grady's earlier revelation had proved, she didn't actually know Mason as well as she'd thought.

Just then, her phone pinged with an incoming text.

Almost reluctantly, Mason broke away, his forehead resting on hers while they caught their breath. She took her phone from her pocket and glanced at the screen, willing the colour to fade from her face and for her legs to start working.

'I need to go. Grady's worrying about where I am.' She wiped at her buzzing lips as if she could erase what had just happened, bucking her hips to free herself from the narrow space between his tempting body and the wall she'd literally backed herself against.

He hadn't fully answered her questions about his feelings, and it really didn't matter how he'd felt back then. He'd walked away, regardless of whether he was pushed or went freely, and, like Lauren, he hadn't had a relationship since. He was as much a danger to her as ever.

What had she been thinking?

Mason Ward might have been the one that got away, but Lauren couldn't allow his words, his kisses or the petrol meets naked flame chemistry they'd just proved was alive and hotter than ever to derail her. Not when, in most of the ways that mattered, he was a virtual stranger.

# CHAPTER EIGHT

BY THE END of the week Mason had replayed the kiss over and over in his mind so many times he'd started to believe that he'd hallucinated it. There had been no time to discuss it then—they'd gone back to the bar and Lauren had only stayed for one more drink before slipping away while Mason had been in the bathroom. Since then, they'd either worked different shifts or only seen each other fleetingly in the ER, each of them too busy to do more than cast wary looks at the other person.

Mason sighed, stretching out his back muscles as he took the lift from the theatres to the hospital cafeteria. He was an hour away from the end of his shift. He'd spent most of it operating and what he really needed to see him through the last part of the day, to help focus his mind away from Lauren and how utterly fantastic it had felt to have her back in his arms, was the miracle of coffee.

Entering the cafeteria, he immediately spotted Lauren ahead of him in the queue, his heart giving an excited lurch. He paused behind her, as close as he could without being obvious. It was close enough that the scent of her floral shampoo tickled his nose and reminded him of her breathy moans as they'd kissed as if the world was ending in the alley the night of Grady's birthday.

Mason tucked his hands into his pockets, out of temptation's way. It wouldn't be a good look to tap her on the shoulder and suggest they continue where they'd left off at the weekend, but that was exactly what he wanted to do.

The final hour of his shift would now seem endless.

Lauren reached the front of the queue and ordered her coffee, requesting an extra shot.

'Make that two of those please,' Mason interrupted. 'And I'll pay for both.'

Lauren began to argue, then she blushed to the roots of her hair.

'I insist, Dr Harvey. I've been trying to buy you a coffee since my first day, if you remember?'

'Thank you, Dr Ward.' She glared his way and then moved aside.

The cashier took his money and he and

Lauren loitered near the barista, waiting for their take-outs. Mason stood beside her, again at a respectable distance. Like Lauren, he pulled his phone from his pocket and pretended to be engrossed in the screen. With their focus on their phones and the silence shrouding them like a laser field, no one would suspect that there had ever been anything intimate between them. Except Mason itched with the urge to tell her how he hadn't been able to stop thinking about their kiss. His body was so restless to move closer to hers and whisper something in her ear, to see if the heat of his breath would make her shudder, the way she'd shuddered against him a thousand times before in pleasure, that he wasn't sure how he could remain so still.

Lauren too was more affected than she seemed. She'd been staring at the same three-word text on her phone for the past two minutes.

Was this torture the vibe of things to come? Were they going to try and ignore each other, pretend to be strangers at work, or would their physical needs get the better of them? To Mason's mind, denial was futile. If last weekend's kiss had proved anything, it was that those needs had taken on a life of their own.

Except he hadn't been completely open to

her enquiries. He'd shied away from confessing how utterly broken he'd been when she'd called things off. He hadn't wanted her to feel guilty. He'd understood her dilemma, that six years ago she'd made the right choice for her by prioritising her family. He only really blamed himself for walking away without a fight.

If only he'd been in the right headspace himself back then. If only he hadn't needed to get away, to go somewhere where he'd be able to be himself, if only it hadn't taken that separation from everything Auckland represented for him to figure out his own priorities.

The barista delivered their coffees, pushed into the same two-cup cardboard holder, an honest mistake since they'd paid together. Lauren stared at it as if she had no idea what to do. Mason scooped up both drinks, smiled his thanks at the barista and ushered a bewildered Lauren out of the cafeteria.

'How is your shift going, Dr Harvey?' he asked, dragging his stare from the way her ponytail swung as she walked. It had felt like silk between his fingers the other night.

'Busy. How about yours?'

'The same.' They paused together at the lifts and Lauren retrieved her coffee from the holder, taking a long sip with her eyes closed as if in bliss.

Heat pooled in Mason's groin at the sight. He had to look away to stop the rush of blood south. Now that he'd tasted her lips again and relearned every soft curve of her body, it was going to be even harder to ignore how much he wanted her. But even more compelling had been the beginnings of her readiness to talk about their past. He'd refused to tear his heart out and lay it at her feet, but the fact that she'd seemed so shocked to learn that he'd called must mean something. Had she too had regrets for the way they'd parted? Had she felt as bereft as he had in the months after they'd split?

The lift arrived. It was empty. Mason hung back to allow Lauren to precede him inside, his stomach hollow with anticipation at the idea they would soon be alone.

When the doors eventually closed, after what seemed like a year, Lauren released a shaky breath.

'You ran out on the celebrations the other night,' he said. 'I'd hoped we could dissect that astounding kiss, but when I returned from the gents you'd disappeared.' There was no point beating around the bush. There was only one thing they needed to talk about and it wasn't work-appropriate small talk.

She turned her gaze on him, her colour high. 'Astounding?' She looked appalled that he'd raised the subject, but also equally fascinated at his choice of descriptor.

He nodded, answering her question with one of his own, because he remembered how much that had once burrowed under her skin. 'You've had better?'

Mason seriously doubted it. Even their first kiss, his gold standard until the night of Grady's birthday, had been a little awkward at first.

At her dazed expression, Mason continued. 'I'm only so confident because, for starters, I was there, and also because Grady told me that you don't date much.'

She shook her head in disgust. 'Some friend he is…'

Mason chuckled. Grady cared about her and always had. The time for Mason's insecure jealousy had been years ago, first time around, but it had rumbled away anyway, fuelled by the spike in testosterone he always experienced around Lauren.

The lift slowed and stopped. A porter wheeled a patient in a wheelchair inside and Lauren scuttled to the opposite corner from him as if she and Mason had been caught in a repeat of that steamy session in the alley. Mason hadn't even noticed that they'd inched closer, but he wasn't surprised. He was a drone to her queen bee.

The elderly lady in the wheelchair smiled at Mason as if she could feel the sexual undercurrents filling the small space. Everyone was young once.

Mason glanced at Lauren and every second they shared the lift stretched taut. She narrowed her eyes and Mason grinned, enjoying himself so much that he no longer required coffee.

'What are you doing?' she hissed the minute the patient had left the lift and they were once more alone.

'I think we should talk about the kiss, don't you?' He hadn't been fully open with her when she'd questioned him about his feelings six years ago, but those few incredible moments in the alley when they'd finally surrendered to their urges had been a great starting point for ongoing honesty. They needed to keep talking, navigate their renewed relationship with candour and maturity. Not that he was in a position to think about anything long-term. He hadn't had a relationship in six years, since Lauren. Clearly, he'd made a mess of that, and he would never toy with her emotions. He didn't even know if he would be a permanent member of GHH staff yet.

'Maybe I'm tired of thinking about it,' she said, taking another mouthful of coffee. 'I just go round and round in circles, because I still don't want a relationship and you and I have been there, done that.'

So why did she look like he'd just snatched away her brand-new kitten, like she wished that something could happen between them, like she was one step away from ripping his scrubs off in this lift and ravishing him?

'I know exactly what you mean. But that kiss, and the way you're looking at me right now, prove that we're going to struggle to be just friends. Do you really want to get so desperate that we embarrass ourselves at work, have sex in the on-call room or burn down the hospital with the flames we generate?'

'Flames?' she mocked, pressing her lips together playfully.

At least she was embracing their usual banter.

'Don't be too overconfident in your abilities.' She smiled and Mason grinned, elated that he'd finally coaxed her radiant smile free. 'You're not in the operating theatre now, and I'm not a besotted twenty-three-year-old.'

'Besotted…? Now there's something I wish I'd known at the time. But if we're making confessions you should know that I'm no longer scared of being honest.'

She frowned, her breaths coming faster. 'About the fact that we've always been too different? That we bicker all the time?'

He shook his head, his gaze drawn to her parted lips. 'About the fact that us being friends feels like a consolation prize that neither of us truly wants. That we can try to ignore our chemistry, but eventually we're going to fail. You know it and I know it.'

Eyes wide, she licked her lips, the gesture almost his undoing. Pity that he had no desire to make things difficult for either of them at work. One embarrassment involving the Ward name was more than enough.

Mason was not his father. He wouldn't fall into the same trap, allow his personal life choices to eclipse his work ethic, become the source of hospital gossip.

'Are you goading me again?' She recovered, her eyes narrowing with suspicion, looking so much like his Lauren that he almost had to look away.

Instead he stepped closer. 'I wouldn't dream of it.'

'Yes, you would. Perhaps you should go out

and find someone to sleep with if you're having such a hard time,' she said, hurling up another defensive barricade as she backed away.

He cast her a sad smile, turning serious. 'If I thought for one second it would help, I'd take you up on your suggestion in a heartbeat,' he said, unable to recall if he even knew how to seriously flirt with a woman that wasn't *this* woman. He hadn't been a saint overseas, but there were unspoken rules about one-night stands.

'Why don't you, then?' she whispered, her body so still she must have been holding her breath.

He braced his hand on the wall of the lift above her head, bent closer, lowered his voice, wishing they were anywhere but at work.

'Because she won't be you, and right now you're all I can see. All I can think about.'

She gasped, her stare ping-ponging between his eyes.

'What are you doing tonight?' He grinned. 'Wanna go for a surf after work, watch the sunset?'

'Really?' Her voice took on a breathy quality that belied her censorious expression. 'You're using our mutual love of surfing in order to get me into bed. That's low.' She rolled her eyes, as if she had way more control over the demands of her body. But he knew the truth as well as he knew her and the struggle he saw in her eyes every time she looked at him. That night in the dark alleyway, that desperate kiss was the closest she'd come to absolute candour.

He laughed, delighted by how much of Lauren's playful side was reappearing. Maybe there was something to be said for that friendship thing after all, except friends didn't usually want to rip each other's clothes off.

Then her pager sounded, saving them from creating a scandal.

She glanced at the screen as if grateful for the distraction. 'It's the ER.' A small frown pinched her brows together. 'There's been a multi-vehicle accident on the Southern Highway. It's going to be all hands on deck.'

Mason nodded, silencing his own pager, which carried the same alert.

'A rain-check then,' he said as the lift doors opened on the ground floor and they dumped their coffees in a nearby bin. There was no time to think about what would happen next for them, now that they were trapped somewhere between friends and lovers.

Duty called, and that meant that they'd have to put their personal lives aside.

## CHAPTER NINE

TWELVE HOURS LATER, after working a double shift to assist with the extra influx of casualties the major road incident had brought in, Lauren feared that she'd never find the physical strength to leave the hospital. Admitting the accident victims, many of them in a critical condition, had created a knock-on effect whereby the less serious cases already waiting in the ER were triaged as lower priority. It had taken most of the night to process the backlog. She was so tired that her legs might not be able to carry her the short walk home.

But, even exhausted, all she could think about, now that she was free to leave the hospital, was Mason.

They'd seen plenty of each other overnight, which he'd either spent in the ER accepting the steady stream of surgical patients she'd referred, or in Theatre. There hadn't been a spare minute for them to discuss how they were going to navigate the complexities of their inescapable relationship going forward. But what there had been were multiple opportunities for them to show that they were in each other's thoughts.

On several occasions Mason had come to the department with some sort of nutritional offering, placing it wordlessly on the desk next to her before going about his business: a sandwich, a coffee, an apple. Lauren had insisted that he crash for half an hour in between surgeries on the sofa in her office, leaving him a bottle of water and some toast for when he woke up.

Now, she pushed through the doors from Minor Injuries to find Mason waiting at the staff lockers for her with two takeaway coffees and a brown paper bag that smelled delicious. She almost sobbed in gratitude. Like her, Mason was still dressed in hospital scrubs, his hair in disarray and his eyes red-rimmed with fatigue. She doubted that he'd had time for a shower, but he'd made time to fetch her breakfast or dinner or whatever meal it was. She'd lost track of the time hours ago.

She took the proffered bag and inhaled the buttery greasy smell emanating from the contents, some sort of toasted sandwich. She was so hungry she'd have eaten the paper bag alone.

'Sorry—' he passed her one of the coffees with an apologetic smile '—it's probably a bit lukewarm by now.'

She shook her head dismissively, taking a grateful sip. 'It's perfect. Thank you. You really didn't have to bring me more food.'

He shrugged, his tired eyes crinkling in the corners in a way that made Lauren want to hug him. 'I know, but us doctors need to look out for each other, right? We're the only ones who understand what it's like.'

A lump lodged in her throat. He was going out of his way to be her friend, but everything he'd said in the lift last night had been true. It felt as if they were fighting a losing battle, especially after that kiss.

Just being around him, with his thoughtful gestures and his unwavering consideration and his charm-loaded smile, was its own form of torture.

He took a swallow of his own drink and adjusted his bag on his shoulder. 'Have you slept at all?'

'No.' She wiped her mouth with the back of her hand and unwrapped the top of the sandwich. 'But I'm headed home now.' She looked away because exhaustion had stolen her ability to think, but there was one thing she did know: she wanted more than friendship with Mason. His openness and honesty were inspiring, liberating and a little bit terrifying. She wanted to jump on board, explore this new dynamic. Once she'd had a decent night's sleep.

'Me too,' he said with a tired smile. 'I'm going to sleep like the dead.'

Her empty stomach growled loud enough that they both laughed. Lauren opened the bag and took a big bite of cheesy deliciousness. 'Oh, wow…' she said, her eyes rolling closed as flavour assaulted her tastebuds. 'This is delicious. Thank you. I love you.'

The second the words were out she almost choked, wishing she could suck them back into her mouth or that Mason had fallen temporarily deaf.

Covering up, she babbled a stream of verbal incontinence with her mouth half-full. 'Are you…um…staying at Murray's place? I meant to ask you at the funeral if you wanted a hand clearing the house of his things. I have the weekend off so I'm free, and I know how hard that process can be because I helped Dad sort through Mum's belongings.'

Her face was hot so she avoided looking at

him, instead slipping into her office and collecting her bag.

Oh, how she wished they were bickering playfully, the way they had in the lift yesterday, but she was too tired and too aware of him to come up with any banter. The old Mason had been hard enough to resist, but this older, self-assured version was ten times hotter—if that were even possible—his diligence and confidence and the way he seemed to look at her as if she was the only woman on the planet a major turn-on.

Mason's stare settled on hers, his eyes serious. Clearly he was too tired to tease her for her slip-up or make some suggestive comment. Part of her half wished he would. Fatigue was a great excuse for making rash decisions and reckless mistakes.

'No. I'm renting in Bushman's Point—great views of the sea, a five-minute walk to the beach. I love it.'

'But that's a thirty-minute drive away.' A stitch of concern pinched Lauren's ribs. He'd had thirty minutes of sleep in the past twenty-four hours. He shouldn't be driving anywhere.

He shrugged. 'I know. The drive helps me switch off from work. By the time I get home I'm ready to head down to the beach for a surf.'

He watched her take a jacket from the hook on the wall and shrug into it. The hood was trapped inside out. Mason stepped close and adjusted it for her.

Lauren swallowed, choked by how cared-for he made her feel. She wanted to kiss him again, to lose herself in the passion she knew would be only one bold move out of reach.

'Thanks,' she said, filling her mouth with warm coffee instead as she flicked off her office lights and headed for the nearest staff exit.

'Where do you live these days?' he asked, the unspoken agreement that they were heading out of the hospital together.

'I've just moved into my own place, a few blocks from here,' she said, her cheeks warm because she was thirty and had only just vacated her family home. She should invite Mason to crash at her place. Excitement hummed in her veins at that idea, probably not her best, but she liked the alternative—him falling asleep at the wheel and driving off the road—even less.

'Until then,' she continued, 'I was still living with Ben and Dad.' She rolled her eyes. 'I know. Late starter.'

Mason smiled without judgement. 'I'll walk

you home then,' he said, eyes front, no innuendo, but also closed-off to any argument.

'There's no need.' Lauren hesitated, not because she didn't appreciate the gesture, although Auckland at five a.m. on a Saturday morning was a relatively safe place, but because she was more worried about him and that long drive.

He shrugged, but his stare was determined. 'I insist.'

Touched by his thoughtfulness, and trying to block out all the times he'd seen her safely home in the past, she cleared her tight throat so her voice wouldn't emerge as a nervous squeak. 'Okay, but only if you crash at my place for a few hours. I'm not having you drive all that way on your bike, on no sleep. It's dangerous.'

He grinned. 'I didn't know you still cared so much.'

She shook her head, a smile twitching on her lips. 'I don't. I just happen to know from the bed co-ordinator that the hospital is full to capacity. We can't take another admission if you fall asleep at the wheel.'

Mason tutted, shook his head in mock disbelief. 'Honestly? You're going to use hospital resource statistics to get me into bed?'

Lauren ignored his chuckle and marched

ahead towards the exit, her heart lighter with the return of their repartee, although at the mention of sex she willed her heart to calm down. The thought of being alone with him, in her house…

She scoffed; she was practically a zombie right now, and likely as alluring.

'I don't have a spare room,' she said, trying to act as nonchalant as possible, 'but my sofa is new and very comfortable.' Then, because she couldn't resist, and she couldn't allow him to have the last word, she shot him a cheeky look. 'And I promise, no funny business.'

His gorgeous grin stretched wide, alarming and enticing. 'Shame, I'm in the mood for some funny business, although I couldn't promise that I wouldn't totally fall asleep on you.'

Lauren almost combusted at the idea of her and Mason naked, tangled up in sheets, hot, sweaty, limbs entwined…

'Good,' She shoved the door open, hoping to find a blast of cooler air to tame her raging internal fires, but Auckland was putting on a show of what promised to be another glorious day, the breeze already warm and slightly humid. 'Then that's settled.'

With the chance of sex dispensed with,

Lauren resumed eating her sandwich, despite the rebellion from her fluttering stomach.

'How are the accident victims we admitted?' she asked after they'd walked a short distance in silence.

He scrubbed a hand through his hair. 'They're all stable. One has been transferred to Neurosurgery, a couple to Orthopaedics.'

'And the six-year-old?' she asked about the last casualty they had admitted together in the early hours of the morning. The little girl had been a rear passenger trapped in one of the vehicles for over an hour. The seatbelt had saved her life, but she'd had abdominal injuries and a crushed arm where the car had rolled. She and Mason had worked for an hour together to stabilise her before he'd whisked her to Theatre.

Mason's stare became haunted, the lines around his eyes deepening. 'I had to remove her spleen. Orthopaedics are still observing her arm, but I'm worried that it doesn't look good.'

Lauren swallowed, understanding the implications and Mason's investment in the patient. It was often the cases of the seriously ill children who came through the door that she found difficult to forget. Just because doctors saw all manner of human tragedy didn't mean that they were unaffected.

'That's hard. I'm sorry,' she said, touching his arm, a gesture that now felt second nature, almost necessary to her existence. 'Let's hope that today brings better news.'

He nodded, his fatigued stare searching hers in an exchange of empathy. That they understood each other's work made some of Lauren's doubts settle, but then Mason seemed to understand everything about her, despite the passing of time. He'd seen her at her worst—sobbing with grief for her mother, overwhelmed by her new role nurturing Ben and wishing that her father's grief would lessen so their broken little family could resume some semblance of normal—and he still wasn't put off…

'Still worrying about me, I see,' he said with a smile that would normally reassure her and break the tension but only inflamed her desire to throw herself at him.

'Occupational hazard,' she replied, pressing the pedestrian crossing button to hide her flush. So she cared about him. She cared about many of her friends and colleagues. That was who she was.

Of course she didn't make out with any of

them as if the continuation of humanity as a species was dependent on it.

'Don't get me wrong,' he added with smug grin. 'I like it. It's endearing.'

'Do you, now?' Without waiting for his confirmation, and too tired to examine the perilous thud of her heartbeat, she walked across the road.

'That was one of the things that drew me to you in the first place, aside from your smarts and everything else.' He waved his hand in her direction, encompassing her head to toe. 'You always accepted me as I am. I never had to pretend to be anything else with you.'

'That's me—Saint Lauren.' Her head spun at his revelation. Did they really need another confirmation of how good they'd been together? And yet they'd still managed to mess it up.

She couldn't deny that she trusted him, wanted him, and, knowing how he'd always managed to bring out her reckless streak, it seemed inevitable that she would act on her desires, especially if he kept on looking at her in his intense way, as if he was learning new things about her all the time.

Arriving at her town house, she sighed, a tired mess of emotions. She twisted the key in the lock, her hands trembling. It would be so easy to stop fighting, to surrender to their chemistry and sleep with Mason one more time. But she would need to be strong enough to keep her emotions in check. They'd let each other down once before, and neither of them needed the complication of hurt feelings right now when their professional lives were so busy and demanding.

She preceded Mason inside, aware of his proximity, every brush of air against her skin as if she were already naked. This was the stupidest idea she'd ever had, inviting temptation personified through her front door. The only saving grace, one she intended to remedy before she collapsed into bed, *alone,* was that she hadn't had a chance to clean her teeth or shower since yesterday.

The hairs on the back of her neck prickled to attention as she led Mason into her barely unpacked living room. The house still had that new house smell. She pulled the curtains closed to block out the rising sun. It was weird to go to bed when the rest of the city were just waking up to the start of a stunning weekend, but they were both used to odd hours.

'Couch—' she pointed out the obvious large sectional sofa, wider than a king single bed '—I'll get you some bedding and a pillow.'

Being in an enclosed space with him made her aware of his eyes on her, every beat of her heart, the gentle rhythm of his breathing.

'Looks comfy enough,' said Mason, seeming relaxed where she felt out of her depth. 'I can sleep standing up, so don't worry.'

But then she hadn't ever brought a man home to this house. She hadn't brought a man home to her father's house since Mason. Her last sexual encounter was so long ago she might not actually remember the moves.

One look at a sexily sleepy Mason was all it took to blast that theory to smithereens as heat pooled low in her pelvis and her breasts tingled eagerly.

No, they were both exhausted. Not the time for making momentous, potentially life-altering decisions. Everything would become clear and manageable after sleep. With any luck, Mason would have left by the time she surfaced so she wouldn't have to deal with him all warm and inviting and barely awake.

Lauren marched to the linen cupboard, an insistent throb between her legs. She thrust a pile of blankets and a pillow at him, her eyes darting around the room at the unpacked boxes. Anywhere but at the man who was about to strip his likely still sublime body, probably down to his boxers, in her living room.

'The bathroom is through there,' she croaked. 'Help yourself to a shower. Towels are in the cupboard.'

'Thanks.' He looked as if he was about to say something important or lean in to put a friendly goodnight kiss on her cheek. But she couldn't allow that; she didn't have the strength to fight her urges and she'd likely jump him. The poor man had been operating all night.

Lauren hurried to the kitchen and poured herself a glass of water then shuffled off towards her bedroom. 'Help yourself to anything you want,' she muttered, walking backwards, her hand finding the doorknob. Then she remembered that there was no lock on her bedroom door, no physical barrier to the temptation to ravish him in his sleep.

Her fatigue had reached delirium level now. She let out an almost hysterical laugh. ''Night, Mason.'

His sleepy smile weakened her knees. 'Goodnight, Lauren.'

She closed the bedroom door and rested her forehead against the cool wood while her heart thumped at her breastbone.

Great idea. She'd invited the man she couldn't stop craving, even though it felt foolhardy and dangerous, to sleep naked on her couch. How on earth was she supposed to sleep through that kind of temptation?

Hours later, she awoke to an unfamiliar sound.

Her heart thumped as she sat up in bed, her hearing attuned to the slightest noise from the living room. Mason. Mason had slept in her living room. Naked. Heat zapped through her nervous system so that she became instantly awake. The clock read eleven-sixteen, the bright sun outlining the edge of the blinds. There was no way she'd be able to get back to sleep now, not when the noise had likely been Mason moving around.

Panic gripped her stomach. Was he leaving? Sneaking out without saying goodbye, as she'd hoped he would?

The idea that he might leave when he'd been the first thing to enter her mind when her eyes opened propelled her from her bed. She rushed to her en suite bathroom and cleaned her teeth. She pinched her cheeks and ran her fingers through her sleep-messed hair in the mirror.

She had no idea what game she was playing, but she was done living cautiously and over-thinking. She'd made enough sacrifices over the years and she didn't want the potential of one more passionate encounter with Mason to be yet another loss.

She padded into the lounge, the new carpet soft underfoot. Her pulse thrummed in her throat. Mason sat perched on the edge of the sofa, a glass of water in one hand, his face illuminated by the screen of his phone.

'Sorry,' he said, placing his phone and glass on the coffee table and standing. 'I didn't mean to wake you.' He rubbed a hand over his stubble-covered jaw. 'I couldn't get back to sleep, but I didn't want to leave and risk waking you up with the noise from the front door. Now I've done that anyway...'

He trailed off, his stare moving down her body to her bare legs beneath the hem of one of the oversized T-shirts she liked to sleep in.

Lauren's half-asleep brain blinked on and off like a faulty neon light as she repaid the favour, taking in his attire, or lack thereof. As predicted, he was wearing nothing but black cotton boxers, his lean, muscular body defined in the slant of light from the edge of the closed curtains.

Her mouth dried. Words formed and then evaporated. He was beautiful, strong, more manly than the younger Mason she remembered. Dark hair dusted his tanned arms and legs and chest. She wanted to objectify the hell out of him, stare at his near naked body until her eyes watered, but she also knew him well enough to know that he would never disrespect her that way. That if anything were to happen between them, and it definitely wasn't wise, she would need to instigate it, just like she had with the kiss.

Remembering how he'd almost made her beg for his mouth on hers, she pressed her legs together and shuddered. That he'd respected her stupid, over-cautious rules made him even more attractive, more irresistible. That he'd confessed his struggles in the wake of that amazing kiss, the evidence of his restraint once more etched into his features now, made her want him even more.

Was that even possible?

She met his gaze. Nervous anticipation churned her stomach. She hadn't felt this jumpy and impulsive since their very first time, which had been after the Medic's Ball during their third year.

He'd romantically booked a room for them at the hotel where the function had taken place. They'd stripped slowly, wordlessly facing each other. 'Are you sure?' he'd whispered against her lips as she'd clawed at him, writhed her body against his, all but begging him to put them both out of their misery.

'Absolutely,' she'd pleaded, kissing him so passionately she'd felt guilty for using every tactic she could to get what she'd wanted: him, inside her, driving them to oblivion.

They'd stayed awake all night, worked their way through a whole box of condoms. It had been the best night of Lauren's life.

'Now that you're awake, I can leave,' Mason said, dragging her mind back to the moment from a past she'd refused to allow herself to recall in too much detail. His voice was gruff from sleep and he looked around for his clothes, sending her pulse into an alarming rhythm.

'It's okay. Once I'm awake, I'm awake. Occupational hazard.' Desperate that he might leave and skittish by how much she was prepared to beg him to stay, she smiled, her cheeks rubbery, trying to calm her nerves and lighten the atmosphere for her own sake. She needed to pull herself together; she was a mature woman, a sexual sophisticate. She wanted him. She'd agonised over her desires enough. It was time to be honest. No emotions, but also no regrets.

'Don't go.' She stepped closer, her mind blessedly devoid of any noise, warning static or the constant compulsion to do the right thing, be responsible.

But the urge to be reckless, to relive how good they'd been together physically just one more time, clawed at her resolve.

His breath came faster, his stare almost silver in the low light. 'Lauren,' he whispered, what looked like the agony of uncertainty of a man on the edge reflected on his face.

Wordlessly, Lauren reached out, placed her hand flat on his chest over his heart, her palm absorbing the rapid pounding and the heat of his skin.

'Are you sure this is what you want?' he said, just as he'd done all those years ago, his rigid body stock-still. 'I don't want you to have any regrets, to make things awkward at work.'

'We're not at work,' she said, her focus blurring with the intensity of watching the struggle on his face. 'You were right…about the flames. I'm tired of denying myself. Tired of overthinking.' She stepped closer until her thighs brushed his, her nipples grazing his chest through her T-shirt. 'I want to be reckless again, just one more time.'

She looked up, pausing a hair's breadth from his lips. She wanted to plead, to say *I know this is going to be so good, but if you could be a little bit rubbish it will help me to keep my feelings out of it, help me to walk away afterwards.*

But it didn't matter how much he rocked her world, they weren't meant to be. They'd proved that last time when they'd let each other down. Her priorities still had to be selfish. She owed herself that much after everything she'd given up to get where she was.

Mason cupped her face, that soul-destroying passion shining from his eyes. She'd almost forgotten its potency. To be trapped in its beam once more sent her body swaying in his direction, until she leaned against him from shoulders to hips.

He traced her lips with his thumbs, as if relearning their shape. 'I've thought about the possibility of this every day since I booked my plane ticket to come home.'

She closed her eyes against the decadence of his confession as she slipped her arms around his waist, clung as if he was the only thing keeping her upright. She couldn't hear how he'd thought about her even before they'd met again. Not when he'd hinted that he'd regretted their split, thought about her over the years, called her less than a year after he'd left.

This had to be casual, a one-off. She was

too set in her ways, too career-oriented to be emotionally derailed again.

'Shh,' she said, surging up on her tiptoes to close the space between his mouth and hers. She wanted to feel, not to think about what his words meant. She wanted a return to that oblivion she'd only ever felt with Mason.

With a groan, he scooped one arm around her waist and hauled her the last millimetre to crush their mouths together.

She parted her lips under his and kissed him unreservedly, free at last to indulge the way she'd wanted to the minute he'd walked back into her life.

They moved in sync, deepening the kiss, tongues gliding together, lips clinging, breath mingling. It felt as if they'd never been apart, only better: new and familiar and truthful. She tangled her hands in his hair, curled one leg around his, all but climbing his body in order to feel close enough.

But did close enough exist? Now that she'd given in, she doubted she'd ever feel satiated. It seemed impossible, but this kiss surpassed the ones in the alley. Heat, hard planes, tantalising bursts of naked skin against naked skin.

She shook, scared that she might not survive this experience.

Mason tore his mouth from hers and trailed

kisses down the side of her neck. 'Are you okay? Cold?'

'No.' She dropped her head to the side on a moan she felt to the tips of her toes, granting him access. She was burning alive, even as she told herself to hold something back.

Mason fisted the hem of her T-shirt and swiped it over her head in one smooth move, dropped it unceremoniously on the floor and allowed his lips to continue their exploration. Her clavicle, her shoulder, her chest.

She slid her hands over his solid warmth, relearning the outline of his broad shoulders under her palms, the contours of his chest, the ridges of his taut abdomen and the silkiness of his skin.

He felt like *her* person, her Mason.

Had it always been this good, an all-consuming drive to touch and stroke and kiss and never stop?

His hands cupped her breasts and her hips jerked. He knew just how to caress her as if they were made for each other, or he'd never forgotten the shape of her body, the places that made her sigh. This man knew her—her weaknesses, her dreams, her body. Surely she could give herself over to this without fear?

She opened her eyes to find him watching her reaction to his touch. Refusing to suffer alone, she stroked him through his boxers. He shuddered under her touch, a sexy groan at the back of his throat. Had he made that sound before? Was she driving him as insane with lust as he was her?

'I want you so badly.' He gripped her hips and shuffled her back towards the brand-new sectional sofa she'd had delivered three days ago.

For a second she wondered if they should move to the bedroom. But she didn't need all of the creature comforts or a fairy tale reunion. She just needed to get past this wonderful, terrible obsession, to prove to herself that them together couldn't possibly be as good as she remembered. With this uncontrollable urge that had taken them both captive managed once more, she could resume her priorities.

She sat on the sofa and he fell to his knees in front of her. Their eyes locked so Lauren felt seen through to her very soul.

'You're so beautiful,' he said, his fingers spearing into her messed-up hair. 'I've thought about this so many times, but my fantasies were rubbish in comparison to the reality of you.'

He raked his stare over her naked body,

bold and unapologetic, as if committing every inch of her to memory.

'I wish we'd started this hours ago,' he continued. 'Half the day has already gone. I've wasted hours sleeping.'

She swallowed, overwhelmed by his heartfelt admission, already mentally agreeing that one time probably wasn't going to be enough for either of them, that they could stretch it to one day, the way they had that first time.

His lips trailed over her skin, his words mumbled there, but clear. 'You are so very hard to forget. Believe me, I've spent six years trying.'

Goosebumps erupted over her exposed skin, his confession slicing into her chest. She couldn't hear this now, not when this was supposed to be purely physical, not when he made it sound as if they'd both had undeclared feelings when they'd split.

Was it possible that he'd felt as deeply for her as she'd secretly felt for him?

She gripped his arms and tugged, pulling him up until he crushed her onto the upholstery, naked chest to naked chest, kissing her once more to block out the questions in her head. Lauren combusted, the heat of his skin and the sexy groan he uttered almost melting her into her new sofa.

It was too good. He'd barely touched her and already she hovered close to climax. His hands roamed her skin, his touch warm and sure as if he recalled every contour of the landscape of her body. His scent filled her nostrils, smothering her senses, imprinting into her mind like a fresh and evocative memory.

His mouth trailed south, finding her nipple so that she dug her nails into his shoulders. 'Mason!' The cry was torn from her throat.

'I know, I know,' he said against her skin as he slid off her underwear while she shoved at the waistband of his boxers, as if neither of them could wait a second longer, as if even with him inside of her it wouldn't be close enough.

Could he possibly know how she felt? Was he equally consumed by this compulsion they had no hope of controlling until it had run its course?

He'd hinted as much, teased her about it, but Lauren had always pushed aside pretty words and promises, preferring hard, irrefutable evidence. Even when people swore they'd always be there for her, things changed beyond anyone's control. People left. Disappeared. Died.

He slipped his hand between her legs, observing her reaction to his touch as if he couldn't look away. All she could do was share his kisses and surrender to his inescapable stare until the desire to have him inside her became unbearable.

'There's a condom in the bedroom,' she said between gasps of pleasure, belatedly realising they should have moved to her bed after all.

'I have one.' He reached for his bag and took protection from his wallet.

'Thank goodness.' She smiled in relief.

He smiled too and she cupped his face, familiarity so strong it knocked the air from her lungs. He pressed a quick kiss to her lips, covered himself and settled his hips back between hers, his jaw taut and his heart thumping against her ribs.

Lauren shifted under him, her bottom lip trapped under her teeth in anticipation. Now that she was seconds away from the fulfilment of her wish, she almost wanted to flee. What if it was too much? Too intense? Too dangerous?

As if sensing the vulnerability shredding her, Mason held her face, tunnelled his fingers into her hair, brushed his lips over hers as he slowly pushed inside.

'I've missed you,' he said, his body shuddering with some kind of momentous effort to hold back.

Her stare clung to his, vision swimming, eyes burning. 'Me too,' she confessed, too drunk with lust and awash with their new code of honesty to guard her thoughts. But it was true. Her sexual encounters these past six years had been woefully few and far between and depressingly superficial. She could trust Mason. They knew each other's bodies. They knew each other's pasts, each other's tender spots. She could truly let go with him. Be herself. Be free.

She gripped his arms, which were braced either side of her head as he rocked into her. Their mutual groans collided in a rush of hot breath and unwavering eye contact that felt way too intimate for a one-night stand. But Mason would always be more to her than that. Their shared history meant he would always have a place in her heart, no matter how well she defended that tender organ.

'It's never been like this with anyone else but you,' he admitted, rocking his hips and snatching another moan from her throat. 'I tried to fight it, believe me, I tried.' He closed his eyes on an agonised wince.

Lauren closed her eyes too, as if by doing so she could block out his candour. 'I know.

Me too.' But sometimes attraction was too strong for a reason.

No matter how good they were together, this could only be about the here and now. The moment. She'd made enough choices putting others first. This time in her life was for her, and her weakness for him had already come at a professional cost, resigning from the interview panel.

She raised her hips to meet him, tugged his weight fully down on top of her and kissed him, silencing further talk. His declarations, while a serious aphrodisiac, brought her too close to the edge of a terrifying precipice.

They could have this one time. It would put the past to rest and cure them of their all-consuming hunger for each other.

But as she shattered into a million pieces, surrounded by, engulfed by and consumed by Mason, she feared that, this time around, sex, even the best sex ever, just wouldn't be enough.

# CHAPTER TEN

SUNDAY MORNING, MASON abandoned the eastern coastal Road, which featured a dramatic view around every bend, and pulled his bike into a familiar car park at Pinnacle Point. He'd forgotten the perfection of a stunning New Zealand summer's day, or maybe it was more beautiful than he remembered because Lauren was on the back of his bike, just like old times.

He kicked out the bike stand and held the weight of the bike steady, braced for the loss of the heat and closeness of her body as she dismounted. Dread twisted his gut. Just like he could easily recall memories of all their firsts—first touch, first date, first kiss—he was also plagued by their impending lasts. Would today be her last ride on his bike? This trip to the beach their last date? He couldn't bring himself to contemplate that being inside her over and over again since yesterday, watching her disintegrate in his arms, his chest full of forbidden and conflicted emotions, might be the last time they would be truly honest with each other.

Because sex had always been their most vulnerable form of communication.

Mason sighed and removed his helmet.

The minute that first time was over, when she'd come to him all warm and flushed from sleep, wearing nothing but a T-shirt that barely skimmed the tops of her thighs, he'd clung to her, trying to reel his feelings back in, out of sight, in case she'd see the evidence of how he felt about her on his face. In case she was horrified and asked him to leave. He *should* have left, taken the time to put his head on straight. Instead, they'd indulged in a joint shower, eaten brunch on her tiny veranda and then went back to bed until this morning, exhausting their supply of condoms. At one stage, when neither of them had been able to admit the sexual reunion was over, Mason had rushed out to the pharmacy for another box.

This morning, when they'd made love for what felt like the millionth time, he still hadn't been able to bring himself to leave. And as if she too never wanted their weekend to end, she'd suggested a ride, citing the benefits of fresh air to clear the sex haze, and he hadn't thought twice about agreeing.

Stupid, stupid, stupid.

Of course one time with Lauren was never going to be enough. Even one weekend with her hadn't sated him in the slightest. Being with her again physically had felt more like coming home than literally *coming home.*

He was so doomed.

He joined Lauren at the lookout point where she'd paused to admire the view, the screech of cicadas in the trees almost deafening. Mason settled at her side, his forearms braced on the railing as he stared out at the volcanic bush-clad cliffs and the small sandy beach below. Their beach.

'Bit of a cheap shot, don't you think,' she said, casting him a look full of mock reproof from under her raised sunglasses. 'Stopping at our beach, the scene of our first kiss.' She bumped his shoulder with hers playfully, her eyes sparkling and her words coming out a little breathless.

'It seemed appropriate.' He stepped closer until their bodies welded together, shoulder to thigh, the physical draw of her overriding any thought of self-preservation. 'I thought you might enjoy the trip down memory lane.'

He dipped his head, brushed her lips with

his, pulling back from actually kissing her. 'And in case today also marks our last kiss, there's a symmetry to it being here too, don't you think?'

She stared up at him, suddenly wide-eyed with an uncertainty that he couldn't allay, no matter how much he might want to. Regardless of how she felt about continuing this fling, he couldn't definitely say he'd be staying in Auckland permanently unless he was successful in his application for the consultant post. And even if he was in that position, Lauren didn't want promises. He hadn't come back to Auckland for her, but things had changed. Like it or not, they'd developed some sort of relationship, even if there was currently no label for what they were to each other. Could he take the consultant job, commit to staying long-term and risk growing closer to her again, risk that she might, yet again, push him away?

'Were you always this romantic?' She kept her face in profile, her hair blowing in the warm breeze, as if she was afraid to acknowledge any of those good times, afraid to see them reflected in his stare. Something inside Mason recoiled. Had she truly had no idea six years ago how he'd felt about her? But then he hadn't recognised it either, until it was too late.

'If you have to ask, then no, I probably wasn't. I guess I had more than one failing as a boyfriend. But, in my defence, you always seemed a little embarrassed by romantic gestures.'

She frowned, glanced his way, quickly returned her eyes to the view. Mason could have kicked himself for killing the mood.

'I wasn't embarrassed,' she said slowly. 'I just struggled to trust my feelings back then, because losing Mum had made me doubt everything. I'm sorry if that's how it came across to you.'

She looked up at him, the face he'd witnessed showing every possible human emotion bar one, perhaps the most profound one—love—shadowed with vulnerability. Mason held his breath, convinced she was about to open up.

'After she died, something in me shut down emotionally,' she confessed, as he'd predicted. He took her hand and she smiled a sad smile. 'We had been so close my whole life and then she was gone. I'd never felt so alone. By the time I met you, I'd already decided that I never wanted to hurt ever again, that pain was directly correlated to deep feelings, to love, and I'd do everything in my power to avoid it.'

Mason drew on a deep well of patience, this moment momentous in its honesty.

'I couldn't articulate all of this at the time,' she continued, her eyes as vulnerable as when she'd come to him yesterday afternoon, 'but I think placing myself in a caregiver role for Ben made me feel as if I was still close to Mum, that she would rest in peace knowing that at least her children had each other. He was so young, and I'd had my childhood with two parents. I was scared that if I left Auckland with you, something terrible would happen and I'd…'

'Be hurt again?' he supplied, his stomach lurching with the realisation that he and Lauren had been destined to fail from the start.

She nodded in confirmation. 'So I stuck with what I knew.'

Mason held her close, his throat thick with emotion and the urge to kiss her until no more doubts existed. Until he'd extinguished the most burning of his questions: Had she loved him?

'I'm sorry if I stifled your romantic gestures because I was messed-up,' she whispered. 'Will you forgive me?'

'There's nothing to forgive. It's like you

said, we're only human; we all have regrets and I was messed-up then too.' They'd both made mistakes and let the other one down. Discussing it might be the first step to moving forward, because surely they couldn't just leave things where they were after that weekend…

Seeing her eyes gloss over, he changed the subject. 'Come on, let's walk down to the beach, see if it's as magical as I remember.'

She sighed, a sound of contentment. 'I loved coming here with you,' she said as he tugged her towards the rugged path that zigzagged down the cliff to their beach. 'It was one of the only places I felt carefree. The hours we spent swimming, talking, just the two of us.'

Mason winced, conflicted that one place could hold such dichotomous associations, some of the best and the absolute worst of their moments. 'We also said goodbye here,' he reminded her, his feelings equally forked. Just as she'd been wary of making herself vulnerable to him back then, she'd also had the power to hurt him, a risk that had actually materialised when she'd called it a day.

She chewed her lip, her stare apologetic. 'Yes, we did.'

Mason kissed her hand. He hadn't brought

her here to rehash their break-up. He'd wanted to reconnect beyond the intimacies they'd shared, to remind her that there had been, and still could be, more to them than two people who were insanely attracted to each other.

They were good together, good for each other.

But where he felt like a different person from the one that had left Auckland and Lauren behind, he couldn't be sure that she was any more ready to commit to a relationship than she had been first time around. Could he put himself on the line again without any certainty that she too had changed? It had hurt enough last time.

They arrived on the sand to find the small beach deserted. They kicked off their shoes and left them perched on a rock before heading down to the water's edge.

The feel of the cool water around his ankles, the sand softening underfoot, settled the worst of his discord. 'You know,' he said, 'after six years working for Medicine Unlimited, the first thing I did when I hit Auckland was take my board out into the Gulf for a surf. I never realised I could miss the sea so much.'

She leaned into his side, a serene smile on her face. 'Was it everything you dreamed?'

'Better than my dreams and almost as good as *our* times on this beach—picnics, bonfires, that time I persuaded you to go skinny-dipping.'

She laughed, then sobered, a frown tugging at her mouth. 'But you're back now,' she said hesitantly, as if the observation had only just occurred to her. 'You're planning to stay. You're...different.'

He was different. He might make the same choices—he didn't regret his experiences overseas—but a part of him, the part newly intoxicated by Lauren after the two incredible days they'd shared, wished he'd never left at all. But then he might not have learned valuable lessons about himself, he might not have become the man he was proud to be today.

Because she was still staring up at him, her eyes tinged with what looked like wonder, and because he could no more fight the compulsion than he could stop the tide, he leaned close, pressed his lips to hers, moved them slowly and lazily.

'Ben and I love to surf together,' she said, her pensive gaze fixed far off. 'Before, you know, he moved away to Wellington.'

Mason pressed his lips to the top of her head, inhaling the scent of her shampoo as her sigh shuddered through her body.

'He's only an eight-hour drive away,' he said, because he could feel how much she missed her brother and hated to see her sad. 'Or an hour's flight. And they have some good surf in Wellington.'

'Mm-hmm,' she mumbled.

'What will you do if you don't get the Head of Department position?' he asked with bated breath. 'Would you ever consider moving anywhere else?'

Framed in relation to Ben living in Wellington, it wouldn't be too obvious that Mason was asking to satisfy his self-serving curiosity. If he couldn't get a job in Auckland, he'd have to move elsewhere himself. He couldn't locum for ever. He wanted to begin building his own professional network, and for that he needed a consultant job.

She stiffened slightly in his arms. 'I don't know… I've never really thought about it. I've put in years of hard work in Auckland, and I guess I always figured that Ben would move back home again after university.'

She pulled back and looked up at him, her face tipping up to his. He kissed her, because he couldn't seem to stop touching her, the press of his lips to hers at first relatively chaste, but then turning inevitably heated.

The sun warmed his back. Her sighs brushed at his lips, enticing.

The urge to lay her on the sand and forget their past baggage and their future uncertainty was almost overwhelming. But this was a popular spot with families and tourists and it was the middle of a Sunday morning.

Had their previous relationship ever been that intense? Was it just that they were older, more certain of themselves, more honest?

He pulled back, breathing hard, his forehead pressed to hers while he tried to rein in his desire to have sex on the beach, just to make sure it was as good as it had been for the past twenty-four hours.

Startling Lauren, he climbed to his feet. 'I need to cool down or we might end up getting arrested.'

Something so good, so addictive, was always going to be tricky to manage. But with Lauren likely no more ready for a commitment than she had been six years ago, could he really trust his feelings? Should he even try to pursue this? He had a consultant job potentially on the horizon. He needed to take inspiration from Lauren, be a bit more cautious, careful that his eagerness to embrace their new physical relationship didn't end up hurting both of them.

He scooped his shirt over his head and removed his jeans. A dip in the ocean might help him to turn off this fierce craving that had only strengthened now that he'd relearned every delicious inch of Lauren.

'Are you mad?' Her jaw was slack with disbelief as she gathered his clothes from the sand and automatically folded them into a neat pile.

'Yep, certifiable.' But he had to do something to keep his hands off her, put some distance between their lips, to take his mind off his dangerous thoughts, feelings. He wanted to know where this was going, when she was still predominantly thinking about Ben.

He strode to the edge of the sea, waded out to waist height and then dived under the waves. The shock of the cold slapped him partway to his senses, as he'd hoped. Tomorrow would begin another busy week at the hospital. He had his interview to prepare for and a heap of admin that needed his attention now that his jet lag had finally abated and the funeral was behind him.

He broke the surface of the water, his feet finding shifting sand as he turned to face the beach. He searched out Lauren, expecting to see her where he'd left her, only she wasn't there. She was behind him, wading through thigh-deep water in her underwear.

Mason froze, his heart leaping. She was magnificent. She'd always had the ability to surprise him. He might not know her thoughts, he might not know if they had any more of a future together this time around than they'd had six years ago, but he knew himself. He knew he wasn't ready to walk away from what they'd shared. He owed it to himself to be one hundred percent transparent.

His blood pounded as he watched her dive under the next wave and then emerge soaking wet, her white underwear virtually see-through and her hair slicked back from her face, like something out of a movie.

With a wide grin, she swam to him, wrapping her arms around his shoulders because she wasn't quite tall enough to touch the bottom. Her breasts emerged above the surface, her nipples visible through the wet cotton, the sight decimating every certainty bar one—how much he wanted her.

'I needed to cool down too,' she said, her legs slipping around his hips under the water, her fingers sliding through his wet hair. 'Then I remembered how much fun the skinny-dipping had been. You make me want to be bad, Mason Ward.'

Before his scattered wits could form speech, she kissed him, a salty rush of cold lips and hot tongues that had him bracing his legs against greater forces than the currents. The sea buffeted them, the waves causing their bodies to undulate closer and closer so that all that separated his arousal from the heat between her legs were two flimsy barriers of soaking-wet cotton.

Every cell in Mason's body urged him to be reckless. It would be so easy, so instinctive to push inside her and figure out the future tomorrow. But they had no condom. And that thing buried deep in his chest that wouldn't be ignored clamoured to be set free.

He pulled back, breathing hard, dragging his gaze from Lauren's pupils, which were dilated with desire.

'Are you okay?' she asked, clinging to his shoulders.

'Laurie, I need to tell you something.' He felt her stiffen in his arms and tightened his grip on her waist. Perhaps she wasn't ready for more than one stolen weekend, but if this was the last time they'd spend together as lovers he owed it to himself to be honest about their past, to discuss where they'd gone wrong and acknowledge that they'd let each other down.

'Six years ago, I think I'd been falling in love with you.' The gnawing in his chest intensified at the look of horror on her face.

She gasped, looking down. 'Don't say that,' she whispered, relaxing her thighs around his hips so she could ease away.

'Why? It's true, although I didn't know it at the time.' Mason clenched his jaw, the sickening rumble of rejection accomplishing what the frigid sea hadn't when it came to his ardour for her.

She shook her head, her dark eyes wide, full of fear. 'Mason…' She pressed her forehead to his, her eyes scrunched closed as if she couldn't bear to witness the impact of what she was about to say.

He braced himself, held his breath, gutted that he'd rushed in too soon and made himself so vulnerable.

'Does it matter? We agreed that we are both focused on our promotions right now. This weekend has been amazing. It was even fun being back on the deathtrap,' she said.

She was letting him down gently, retreating to her comfort zone after letting her hair down. Trouble was, he wasn't a pastime. She couldn't dip in and out when she needed a thrill and he couldn't go back to being the man who hadn't known his true self.

Lauren's fear of being vulnerable magnified his own doubts.

He'd been so fixated on trying to make sense of the mess his parents had made back then, so accommodating when she'd dumped him on this very beach, it hadn't even occurred to him to fight for them, to dissect the depth of his feelings, to not give up on the idea of him and Lauren so easily.

Then, like now, he'd obeyed her rules. Aside from that one time he'd called the ER, he hadn't contacted her following the clean break she'd made sound so easy. He'd taken his broken heart, thrown himself into work, joined Medicine Unlimited. One placement had led to another and another, each overseas location easier to exist in because there were no expectations beyond doing his job. He could be himself, be heartbroken Mason and then, after some time, just career-focused Mason. He'd made his own mark—grown into the man he'd always wanted to be.

And that man knew what he would and wouldn't tolerate.

'I understand,' he said, pressing his lips to hers in a chaste kiss before wading them both into the shallows.

He didn't want to hurt her again, or push an agenda that she just wasn't ready for, but he also wanted to be true to himself. She looked up at him warily and he cupped her cold cheeks in his hands. 'The thing is, Laurie, you were right earlier. I have changed. I'm not going to pretend, to take your friendship and the occasional benefit when it's on offer, and I'm not going to sell myself short either. I'm not that man you dumped any more. It matters to me. I know who I am now. I want to be honest with myself, and with you.'

He moved aside and she stopped him with one hand on his arm.

'I'm sorry.' Her stare glistened with emotion. 'Sorry for the cold and logical break-up speech I gave you back then. Of course your feelings mattered. I want you to know that I felt terrible for letting you down, knowing that, either way, I'd have to disappoint someone. And at the time I couldn't bear for it to be Ben.'

He nodded, wanting to state the obvious, that she should always please herself first, but they'd both been dealing with some heavy stuff six years ago. They'd both needed to focus on starting a physically and emotionally demanding job, becoming doctors, building their brand.

'We each had to do what was right for us,' he said, conflicted. Maybe bringing her here hadn't been his best idea. Maybe he'd rushed it, maybe the nostalgia had caused him to mix the past and the present. Maybe they would never be on the same page. 'I guess I just don't want to make another mistake,' he added, shrugging on his T-shirt.

She looked down, gnawed at her lip. 'Of course. Me neither.' She plastered on a brave smile. 'Good thing tomorrow is the start of a new week.'

He'd been referring to the past, the mistake he'd made by letting her go so easily six years ago, where she was clearly talking about this weekend as if she already regretted it.

If that was how she felt it was better he knew it now, before he became too heavily invested. She was doing him a favour and, no matter how heavy the boulder of disappointment that sat in his chest was, it would be nothing compared to how he'd feel if he once more allowed feelings for her to develop, only to have his heart broken again.

Now he just needed to find a way to be okay with them returning to being friends.

# CHAPTER ELEVEN

THE FOLLOWING WEEKEND, the Senior Auckland Health Staff Forum was being held at the Bluewater Bay Winery Estate on Auckland's Waiheke Island, a forty-minute ferry ride from the mainland across the Hauraki Gulf.

Lauren entered the large function room, the venue for the evening's social event, her stomach twisting into knots of desperation to see Mason and to get him alone.

After things had turned rapidly sour that day on the beach, they'd dressed in pensive silence and he'd dropped her at home. Lauren had been so confused, so overwrought by his confession that he'd been falling in love with her when they'd split up, that she hadn't known what to say to him to make things right. Since then, they'd barely seen each other. Mason's week had been filled with extended interviews and social gatherings for the consultant appointment and Lauren had distracted herself from the mess they'd made by succumbing to their physical attraction by finally unpacking all of her moving boxes during her time off.

They'd texted each other, conversed about patients at the hospital, they'd even run into each other in the cafeteria again, but, unlike the time before when they'd flirted so hard she'd almost dragged him into an empty conference room and ravished him, their exchange had been polite and impersonal.

What a difference a week made. After she'd finally admitted how much she wanted him, she'd started to feel as if some missing piece of her had slotted back into place. It made sense. Mason was a huge part of her past, his significance even more marked now that she knew he'd had deep feelings for her back then.

She swallowed hard, choking down her regret. If she'd known at the time would it have made a difference? She stood by her decision to be there for Ben. He was her only brother and she loved him. But what if she'd also been just a little bit selfish six years ago? What if she'd gone with Mason as planned, travelled for a while? What if, instead of breaking things off and then trying to forget him, she'd kept in touch, tried to make a go of a long-distance relationship? What might her life now look like?

Would they have fallen in love? Would they still be together? Married? Have children?

Nausea threatened—she could no longer lie to herself and pretend that she wasn't in serious trouble where Mason was concerned. She frantically searched the room for a friendly face, spying Grady in conversation with Helen Bridges. Desperate for a distraction from her thoughts, she headed in their direction.

Most of the staff attendees, including Helen and Grady, were gathered on the winery's expansive veranda, which boasted a breathtaking vista of the vineyards and olive groves with a backdrop of the distant sea views, in order to take advantage of the last rays of the day's sun.

'I'm sorry again that I had to withdraw from the appointment panel,' Lauren said to Helen with a mental wince. 'I do hope my absence hasn't disrupted the process this week.'

Helen smiled reassuringly. 'Don't worry. My recruitment operations run like clockwork. We missed your youthful enthusiasm, of course—you were the youngest of the group by far—but the rest of us met this afternoon to discuss the shortlisted candidates. One or two of them are head and shoulders above the rest—exactly the right pedigree, if you know what I mean. So unless they botch their final interviews later this week, all that remains is picking the best fit and rubber-stamping the appointment.'

Lauren forced her expression to remain politely neutral while curiosity and protectiveness boiled in her blood. Was Mason one of the two in the running, or was he being unfairly judged on the basis of Murray's mistake?

'By pedigree you mean the right aptitude and surgical skills, of course?' Lauren softened her accusatory tone with a smile. Why was she being so confrontational? That wasn't like her at all.

'Of course,' said Helen, slightly taken aback. After a few more minutes of small talk, the woman smiled and made her excuses, heading to another group to network, the main purpose of these forums.

Left alone with Grady and her own thoughts once more, Lauren shivered. What would Mason do if he didn't get the job? Would he leave Auckland again, head back overseas when there was nothing more to keep him there?

And where would that leave Lauren? Would she watch him go before they'd even had a chance to reconnect properly, to see where their relationship could lead? Not that she could call the current frigid state of affairs a relationship, but that was all her fault. She'd been so overwhelmed by the sex, bewildered by how quickly she'd imagined them picking up where they'd left off that she'd frozen at Mason's confession, retreating back into her safe zone like a hermit crab hiding in its shell.

'The talk is that the Scottish guy is the favourite,' said Grady, reminding her of his presence. 'Although Helen can't be left in any doubt who you'd have favoured if you were still on the panel.'

'I don't know what you mean. I'd have been completely professional and impartial, as you well know.' She looked away from his far too perceptive stare, her feelings churning between relief and confusion. If Mason left Auckland there would be a natural break to this thing they'd started, just like last time. Only she'd become horribly invested in him staying around.

'Anyway, it's really not my business any more.' Lauren sighed, wishing she could escape to the room she'd booked on the estate to sort out her feelings in private. She'd survived without Mason for the past six years, so why did the idea of him leaving again, finding a consultant post elsewhere, make her feel as if she'd just been punched in the stomach and couldn't catch her breath?

'You know, there's a bit of a rumour circulating,' Grady said. 'About Mason.'

She levelled her stare on her friend, her defensive hackles once again raised high. 'I hope it's got nothing to do with that ancient scandal involving his father.' She dropped her voice to a hissed whisper. 'It was nothing to do with Mason in the first place. He's perfectly qualified for the consultant position in his own right, more than qualified. I know, I've seen all of the candidates' CV's and…'

She trailed off, finally registering the morbid fascination in Grady's expression. She was busted.

'And you're sleeping with him again,' he stated. 'That's why you had to resign from the interview panel.' There was no judgement in her friend's voice, only concern in his eyes.

Lauren's jaw dropped, face aflame. 'Not that it's any of your business, but I resigned *before* I slept with him. How did you know? Does the whole hospital know? Are people talking about us? It could damage Mason's chances at the surgical consultant post and that's not fair.'

He deserved as decent a shot as the next candidate. In her opinion he was the best man for the job.

Grady looked sheepish. 'I called around to your place Saturday evening after my shift with a Chinese takeaway as my parents had Molly. I thought you could do with a hand unpacking some boxes. I saw his bike parked outside.'

Lauren's veins filled with heat of a different kind as she recalled exactly what she and Mason had been doing Saturday evening. Then she analysed her earlier reaction to the idea that Mason would be unfairly judged to have done something…inappropriate. The same blood burning hot only seconds ago ran cold.

She was way more invested in him than for a colleague she'd had the best sex of her life with. She'd started to develop feelings for him again.

No wonder she'd freaked out after he'd confessed that he'd been falling in love with her. Then, like now, sadness and frustration and grief for the missed opportunities stung the backs of her eyes.

'Actually,' continued Grady, oblivious to

her turmoil, 'the gossip has been more speculative than damning. People who remember that you two were once an item are wondering if you're together again, that sort of thing. I'm not the only one who was around when you were med students.'

Lauren rolled her eyes. 'Since when do you take any notice of hospital gossip?'

'Since it involves my friend,' said Grady. 'A friend who hardly ever dates, but is now so heavily involved in a relationship that she's being defensive with colleagues. A friend I'm concerned about being hurt again.'

He was right. Mason had hurt her in the past, but, unbeknown to her, she'd also hurt him. At the time, for self-preservation, she'd shut out the possibility that they'd been way more to each other than either of them had confessed. But, as she'd said to Mason on the beach, that was in the past. He wasn't in love with her now.

Fighting the urge to cry, Lauren met Grady's astute and sympathetic stare.

'You're falling for him, aren't you?' he said.

Lauren blinked, sniffed, tossed her hair over her shoulders. 'Don't be ridiculous. We had one night together and now we're barely on speaking terms.'

Was she falling in love with him? He'd only

been back in Auckland a matter of weeks and already her life was almost unrecognisable—motorbike rides, almost having sex on the beach, professional inconsistency.

As if she'd subconsciously always known his location, her gaze darted to Mason on the other side of the room near the buffet table. Her breath hitched at the sight of him, the urge to make things right between them almost overriding every other rational thought. How could he possibly mean so much to her after such a short time? How could she allow him to creep back under her guard, when nothing was certain or planned or decided? She was more exposed, more vulnerable now than she'd been back then. Because the feelings twisting her into knots were momentous compared to the ones she'd fought six years ago in order to be able to let Mason go.

'Why aren't you two speaking?' said Grady, drawing her back from the edge of a terrifying drop. 'You know you can tell me anything.'

She deflated. 'It's complicated, but the gossipmongers are wrong. We're not back together.'

They weren't anything.

'If it's complicated, shouldn't you be over there, untangling it?'

Lauren hated Grady's hesitant smile. It contained too many emotions, the same emotions scrambling her usually rational decision-making processes: a hint of fear, presumably for her being hurt once more, a sprinkle of hope that maybe, this time, she and Mason might make a better go of it and Lauren would finally address the gaping hole in her personal life.

'I don't know any more. I don't have all the answers.' But what if she'd correctly identified her feelings? What if she could work through the fear of losing him from her life once more and meet Mason halfway to this new mature, self-assured and honest relationship?

Didn't she deserve to at least give it some consideration, just like she deserved her professional success?

'I'm no expert,' Grady interjected, 'but what if Mason wants to uncomplicate it too?'

Did he? She had no idea because, stupidly, she'd been so caught up in her own past hurt and her own muddled feelings that hadn't asked him how he felt. She'd just clung to what she'd known, declared it a sound strategy and stuck to her plan.

She shrugged. 'Perhaps it's just better to concentrate on our careers.' Mason's association with her had already put him back at the centre of hospital speculation.

'Translation: you're too scared to even give the possibility a chance,' Grady concluded. 'This is classic you, Lauren. You plan everything, but some things should just be felt, not orchestrated.'

Perhaps realising that he was overstepping a boundary, he softened. 'Well, I'm sorry that it didn't work out. That's a real shame. For a while there, you had… I don't know, a glow about you; something was definitely different. Sorry I brought it up.'

Lauren nodded, choked that she had a good friend in Grady, but scared that the *glow* would be gone for ever if she wasn't brave.

'I think I will explore the buffet,' she stated, raising her chin with a bravado she didn't feel. 'I'm hungry.' Actually, she felt the exact opposite, but she needed to clear the air with Mason.

Grady's gaze flicked in Mason's general direction. 'Good idea.'

Lauren smiled, squeezed Grady's arm and headed inside. Mason had moved to the far side of the buffet table. He was dressed in a casual shirt, which was open at the neck, a place she knew smelled like him and that when she buried her face there, his chest hair tickled her cheek. His dark hair looked damp on the ends as if he'd been for a swim or not long emerged from the shower.

He made her eyes water and her legs wobbly.

Professionally, she'd never faltered in her choices. But what if her personal decisions had been, and still were, shaped by fear? What if she'd stopped listening to her instincts the day her mother died? Was that truly how she wanted to live the rest of her life? Part of her had never moved on. She'd never given another man a chance after Mason. It was easier to barricade her heart than risk it being damaged again. Didn't she owe it to herself, now more than ever, to be honest about her feelings?

They spoke to her. Yelled. Demanded action.

She headed across the room, her steps growing more sure-footed. Because being too close to him would remind her of the weekend and what it had felt like to be back in his arms, and remind her of how they'd parted Sunday evening, Lauren placed the food-laden table between them.

'How are you finding the forum, Dr Ward?' she asked, picking up a plate and placing a single cucumber-based vegan hors d'oeuvre on top. Her hand shook. She hated cucumber. Now she'd have to carry it around the room pretending to eat it until she could discreetly cast it aside.

'Very informative, Dr Harvey,' he answered, tossing a grape into his mouth, his eyes on hers for a second longer than was appropriate for polite, professional conversation. But, unlike when he'd been inside her, his handsome face and emotive stare an open book, she couldn't read him right now.

Was he angry that she'd been scared enough of their connection to withdraw again? Perhaps he'd already moved on, declared her a lost cause.

Her throat became so tight with regret for the wasted years she feared she might pass out.

She forgot all of the things she wanted to say. All she could think about was how much she wanted to hurl herself at him, to apologise, to spend another night relearning all there was to know about Mason physically and discovering new things about the man he'd become.

A man who'd once loved her.

Mason moseyed around the end of the table in her direction, examining the food selection on offer.

'Are you staying the night at the winery?' she asked, somehow keeping her voice low but casual.

She shouldn't be thinking about the sleeping arrangements, how far away from her room his might be. She was getting ahead of herself.

'No, I brought my bike over,' he said, his stare still on the food as if he found the gourmet vegetarian sausage rolls fascinating. 'I'm leaving soon for the last ferry. You?'

The flood of disappointment reverberated through her bones until she almost crumbled. 'I…have a room booked. I'll be on the first ferry in the morning.'

He raised his head, his stare latching onto hers at last.

Lauren's stomach fluttered. She stepped closer, uncaring that they were in a room full of colleagues. 'Can we talk?'

'Sure.' Mason shrugged, but his penetrating gaze held hers.

'Grady knows about us,' she whispered, toying nervously with the single hors d'oeuvre on her plate. 'He saw your bike parked outside my place last weekend.'

Mason cast her a speculative glance. 'We had sex, Lauren. That doesn't really constitute an us.'

Lauren winced, ignoring his statement. She didn't want this to be over, but what did he want?

'There's more.' She kept her voice low so they wouldn't be overheard. 'There's some gossip going around that my withdrawal from the appointment panel is because we're a couple again.'

His lack of reaction spiked her anxiety. His stare was cool ice-blue, but of course he'd be concerned about hospital tittle-tattle affecting his chances for the consultant job.

'I want you to know,' she said, 'that I'll do everything in my power to assure these rumours don't negatively impact your chances for the post. It's not fair. We haven't done anything wrong.'

'Lauren—' he stepped deliberately closer, so she was bathed in his delicious scent '—I don't care about idle gossip.' He reached for another sausage roll, even though he already had three that were untouched on his plate, his gaze locked on hers. 'If I don't get the job it will be because they have a better candidate. But, more importantly, if my suitability for the post is so precarious that some irrelevant rumour will go against me, then Gulf Harbour isn't the workplace for me.'

Lauren's mouth dried. Why did she suddenly feel naive and unsophisticated, when Mason was all sexy confidence and self-awareness, twice the man he used to be?

He didn't move away, and her heart battered her ribs as if trying to escape the searing, searching look in his eyes. 'Besides, we're not a couple, are we?'

All she could do was shake her head mutely, because she couldn't bring herself to ask if he'd want them to be.

'So, there is no problem.' He shrugged and Lauren wanted to leap up onto the table and announce their innocence to their assembled colleagues for Mason's sake. Only she was guilty of wanting him, she had slept with him when she shouldn't have and she'd do it again in a heartbeat.

'No, except…' She stared at him, blocking out the room, full of hospital bigwigs, as if they were alone on their beach again. 'I don't know what this is, I just know that I don't want it to be over.'

His eyes flicked between hers as if he couldn't trust her words.

'I'm sorry,' she blurted, 'if I dismissed what you told me on the beach last weekend. I was completely taken aback, because you were right. It does matter. It matters to me very much.'

'Does it?' His stare hardened.

Lauren nodded. 'I wish I'd known how you felt back then.'

'Would it have made a difference?' Sparks danced in his eyes and she wanted to touch him so badly, to kiss away the vulnerability she saw there, that she clattered her plate onto the table with a trembling hand.

She swallowed, because the past was gone, but she wanted to believe that she wouldn't have pushed him away if she'd known his feelings. 'Neither of us will ever know, will we?'

She wanted to be honest, as honest as he'd been with her. 'But, whatever this is—friends, more than that—I don't want us to mess it up this time.'

He was quiet for so long Lauren worried it was already too late. Then he stopped a passing waiter and handed over his laden plate. 'I've lost my appetite,' he said. 'I think I'll head down to the ferry, return to Auckland.'

His stare carried so much absolution and heat and promise that she shuddered, too aware of every fibre of her clothes against her skin.

How could he do that? Say one thing aloud and another thing entirely with his eyes? But she heard every unspoken word.

He checked his watch. 'It leaves in twenty minutes.' He looked up. *Come with me.* 'Goodnight, Dr Harvey.'

He spun away and strode to the exit, never looking back.

Lauren dithered for a split second, hating herself for second-guessing the best relationship of her life, the only relationship she'd ever given half a chance. She worked hard as a professional woman. Why was she selling herself so short when it came to her personal life? Her career, her promotion mattered, but did it have to mean everything?

With her head held high, she strode from the function room, chasing after Mason, chasing the liberating honesty they seemed determined to embrace. In her room, she quickly gathered the few belongings she'd bothered to unpack and headed out into the night, into the reckless unknown.

Mason waited outside the winery's floodlit entrance. His eyes lit up when he saw her emerge and something bold and carefree bloomed inside Lauren.

Wordlessly, Mason fastened the strap of his spare helmet under her chin, pressed a hard kiss that tasted like relief to her mouth and then leaned forwards so she could slide behind him onto his bike.

With the wind snatching at her hair as Mason rode to the ferry terminal, another thought occurred. What would she do if she fell in love with Mason Ward a second time? This time she knew it would be harder, deeper. It would take over her soul. And there was just no plan for that eventuality.

# CHAPTER TWELVE

THE NEXT MORNING, Mason awoke before dawn, reaching for Lauren automatically, as he had every night since their weekend together. Only unlike those intervening nights, when his arms gripped fresh air and his stomach sank that she wasn't there, asleep at his side, this time his hands met warm, soft, fragrant skin.

Half-asleep, she moaned, reached behind her to grip the back of his neck and twist his hair between her fingers. He dragged her close, burying his face in her hair, kissing the side of her neck, cupping her breasts in his palms until he had her full, undivided attention.

'Is it morning already?' she said, turning in his arms. She pressed her lips to his and lifted her thigh over his hip.

'Not yet, but I never want morning to come, because when it does we'll have to leave this bed, shower and go to work.' He dragged his mouth from the corner of hers, down her neck and across her chest, lifting her breast to his lips.

She sighed, her hips moving against his, driving him to distraction. But he wasn't distracted. His head was full of Lauren. His whole being was full of Lauren.

Her scent covered his skin, her voice and her laughter occupied his head and pleasuring her had become his number one priority. For the first time in his life, he feared that he would never be able to stop touching her, that he'd be irresponsible enough to be late for work or even not turn up at all.

He moved his mouth south, kissing her ribs and her stomach and then between her thighs, filling his senses with her in order to make it through a long day of enforced abstinence.

He moved back up to kiss her lips as he reached for a condom. She helped him, the process slowed by the kisses they couldn't seem to stop, even for a second.

Their tongues tangled as he finally pushed inside her. But instead of moving to the rhythm that his body and Lauren's hungry eyes demanded, he stilled, holding himself deep inside her while they kissed and kissed and kissed.

'I'll want to kiss you when I see you later at work,' he said, gazing down at her swollen lips and pleasure-glazed eyes.

'Me too.' She bucked her hips, taunting him, but still he barely moved.

Instead he pushed her wild hair back from her exquisite features and kissed each of them in turn, the tip of her nose, her closed eyelids, her cheekbones and chin.

'I'll want to lure you somewhere private,' he said, peppering her lips with tiny pecks, 'and make you moan until you look at me, just the way you're looking at me now.'

'Me too,' she whispered, her fingers digging into his shoulders while she ran her lips over his jaw and down his neck.

*I'll want to tell you that I'm in love with you again,* he said, but this time only with his eyes, as he rocked into her and stared down at her and kissed her lips, over and over.

His fertile imagination saw her *me too* in the depths of her stare, heard it in the way she said his name again and again, felt it as she climaxed, clinging so tightly to him with her arms and her legs and her hands that he wondered if they'd actually become one entity with two hearts beating a matching rhythm.

He lay on top of her for long breathless seconds after it was over, the words a lump in his throat. He couldn't just blurt out his feelings and then they'd leave for work. He had no idea how she felt about starting up a relationship again. He understood the fears that had held her back last time. He'd clearly had his own reservations. Why else had it taken him so long to realise how he'd felt about her six years ago?

She'd been open yesterday, showed how much she cared about him by coming to his defence over the gossip she thought might unsettle him, given his father's behaviour in the past. She'd even admitted her confusion and her desire for them to see where this could go. Mason knew these were huge steps for her, given that their previous wreck of a relationship was the most serious one either of them had attempted.

He rolled to lie by her side while they caught their breath. Her hand stroked his chest. His fingers played with her hair. He needed to give her some space, but how would he do that when she felt essential to his existence, like air or water? He certainly couldn't rush to confess his feelings or put her under any pressure. He could be patient. Lauren was worth the wait.

Resolved to reassure her, but also needing

to admit his part in the mistakes they'd made, he pulled her close. 'Laurie?'

'Mm-hmm?' she answered, still groggy and replete from pleasure.

'What I didn't say last night at the function was thank you for looking out for me.' He pressed a kiss to her neck and she snuggled closer.

'You're welcome. It's like you said, we need to look out for each other.'

'But you don't need to worry.' She had enough going on with Ben and her promotion. 'I meant what I said about not caring if people can't see the real me.'

'Okay.' She turned to face him and pressed a kiss to his lips, one he could easily become lost in, if only there were more hours in the day.

He stroked her hair back from her flushed cheeks. 'I wasn't blameless in messing up what we had, you know. After everything that happened with my father, I was sick of being Mason Ward, sick of the expectations and everyone watching me, waiting for me to slip up too. When my mother left, it was easier for me to go where no one knew me, where I could start again, be myself and focus on being the kind of surgeon I wanted to be. Not some guy from surgical royalty perched on a wobbly pedestal. I watched my mother run away, start over, and I thought, why not? Of course I hadn't planned on staying away so long, but then one job led to another and I became increasingly removed from this place, from you, from the idea that you'd moved on and I'd let you go so…easily.' He sighed. 'Until I felt comfortable in my own skin, certain of my own abilities and who I was… I couldn't face coming back, only to be rejected again, so, like my mother, I too took the safer route and stayed away.'

And although she'd been the most constant person to believe in him back then, and that should have been enough for him to take a risk, she hadn't believed in *them*. But surely if he gave her time, if he showed her his feelings, she'd find her way there? Part of him didn't want to be patient. He wanted to shout his feelings from the rooftops. They'd already missed out on the past six years because they'd both been too wrapped up in other stuff to be honest about the way they'd felt, not that she'd ever admitted she'd been in love with him. But he didn't care about the past any more. He only cared about the present and his future with Lauren.

'How are you feeling about how your interview went?' she asked.

'It will be what it will be,' he said, holding her tighter. He hadn't yet told her that he'd received a different job offer via email last week. He'd been head-hunted for a consultant job in his old Australian stomping ground. He planned to tell her once he knew about the Gulf Harbour position, a part of him scared that she might use the news as an excuse to withdraw from him again, encourage him to take it without giving them a chance.

Doubts pounded in his temples. He wanted her to trust him with the important things: her feelings, her private life, her heart, but then he hadn't completely trusted her with his news either.

'What will you do if the job goes to someone else?' she asked, her body stiffening the slightest fraction.

He didn't want his answer to freak her out, so he hedged. 'I don't know. Keep locuming. Look for another job. I haven't really given it too much thought.'

Lauren chewed at her lip.

'What if they're stupid enough to pass you over for the Head of ER?' he asked in return. 'Would you go for a promotion elsewhere?'

'I don't know,' she whispered. 'It's not as easy for me to just up and leave for greener pastures. I have Ben, Dad. Whereas you're free to work wherever you want.'

Mason heard what she didn't add, that she still had the same responsibilities she'd had six years ago, the ones she'd chosen over him.

But there was no way he wanted her thoughts going down that track.

Changing the subject, he said, 'Let's go away for the weekend, somewhere romantic. We can take the bike, find somewhere to risk skinny-dipping again.' If his plan materialised perhaps by then she'd be ready to hear his feelings for her, ready to admit her own.

She laughed, her eyes alight with satisfying excitement. 'Where will we go?'

He nuzzled her neck, drawing out another of her contented sighs. 'You just leave all of the logistics to me. I've checked the roster. We both have next weekend off. Do you have plans?'

She shook her head, gazing up at him with dreamy eyes that settled most of his doubts.

'Good. Then I'll whisk you away from it all.'

That was what they needed. To spend time together away from work, to fall in love all over again, only this time they could hopefully both enter into a brave new relationship without fear.

# CHAPTER THIRTEEN

THE FOLLOWING FRIDAY, after a satisfying week of work, where she'd discovered that she'd been awarded the Head of Department promotion, and five blissful nights of falling asleep entwined with Mason, Lauren had been looking forward to celebrating on their romantic weekend away. Instead, her stomach writhed into a tight knot of trepidation as she heard Mason turn the key she'd given him in the lock of her front door.

Now she had to tell him that she couldn't go away with him this weekend.

She folded a T-shirt and tucked it into her weekend bag, dread dragging at her posture. Mason was going to be disappointed. She was disappointed. But surely he'd understand? After all, they were both fully aware of how life sometimes just happened.

Mason appeared in the bedroom doorway, his slow and sexy smile ripping Lauren to shreds so all she could do for a second was stand frozen to the spot and stare. He'd changed from work clothes into jeans and T-shirt. He looked delicious. Everything inside Lauren clenched. He was so handsome, a brilliant surgeon, a good, kind and caring man.

Because she couldn't stay away from him for a moment longer, she rushed over to him, met him halfway across the room. Their lips collided, their kiss a storm of passion and the desperation of two people who hadn't touched for twelve hours too many.

'I've wanted to do that all day,' he breathed against her lips, his glazed stare zigzagging between her eyes. 'How can I miss you when I see you every day?' Without waiting for an answer, he cupped her breast through her shirt as he backed her up towards the bed where they fell into each other's arms. His thumb teased her nipple and she forgot that she'd had a bad day at work, forgot that she'd need to let Mason down about their trip, almost forgot her worry for Ben and her impending departure for Wellington.

'I missed you too, so much,' Lauren managed as Mason groaned and trailed kisses down her neck. He covered her body with his,

his hips fitting between her legs, his hands in her hair, tilting her face to his kiss.

Lauren's head swam with arousal. Oh, how she wanted to block out the world, her responsibilities, block out reality for a couple of days and immerse herself in the two of them: Lauren and Mason. It didn't matter where, she'd be happy to stay in this bed all weekend if it meant she had a hope of quenching her insatiable need for him. Her flight wasn't for another two hours; there was time for this, but if they ended up naked she'd become sidetracked.

Reluctantly, she pulled her lips from his. 'Wait. Wait,' she said as his hand delved inside her top, curling around her ribs and heading for the clasp of her bra. 'I need to talk to you.'

Her shove at his shoulders was pathetically weak, her hips still writhing against the hard length of him. But then he sobered, looked down at her with such tenderness and devotion she almost sobbed.

'I heard about the patient you lost,' he said, stroking her hair back from her face. 'I saw Grady. I'm sorry.'

She nodded, too grateful for his support and understanding to do more than blink away the sting in her eyes and shuffle away from him so she could think straight.

He lay on the bed next to her, his head propped on one hand while the other hand caressed her hip. 'You don't have to shoulder everything alone, you know. I understand what it's like. I'm here for you.'

She nodded, squeezed his hand, showing him that she agreed. 'I know. It's not that.'

Lauren, as much as the next person, understood how life carried no guarantees. How it could be brutal. People died, like her mother; or they made mistakes, like Mason's father, or they let other people down, the way she and Mason had done in the past.

'What is it?' He sat up, his stare full of concern.

She stood, paced her bedroom to the wardrobe and tugged a sweater from a hanger, nerves stalling her breath. 'I can't go wherever it is you had planned this weekend.' She kept her eyes downcast while she folded the jumper, only looking up once she'd placed it in her bag. 'I'm sorry.'

His brow crinkled in confusion. 'Why not? Do you need to work?'

Lauren shook her head, regret gripping her throat. 'No, it's not that. Ben called earlier. He's sick.'

Mason stood, moved to her side and took both of her hands in his. 'Seriously sick? Is he okay? What is it?'

She looked away, his worry for her brother pressing down on her chest. 'No, just some horrible virus that's going around his hall of residence.'

'Oh, that's good.' Mason breathed a sigh of relief and then added, 'Well, you know what I mean—it's good that it's nothing serious.'

Lauren nodded, refusing to contemplate the kind of panic she'd be in if Ben had been seriously ill. 'I'm flying to Wellington. My plane leaves in just under two hours.' Lauren couldn't bear to witness any dejection he might feel, so she fussed with the zip on her bag. 'I'm sorry about this weekend. Can we… reschedule?'

Mason frowned, walked to the window in silence.

Lauren chewed at her lip, awash with guilt and frustration. After their busy week, she'd been looking forward to spending time alone with Mason. But Ben needed her. Their father was in Australia on a work conference. There was no one else. She and Mason could go away the next time their rosters coincided in a weekend off, whenever that would be…

'Does Ben want you there?' Mason's voice

was quiet, careful, his back to her so she couldn't read the expression behind his tone.

'He didn't ask me to come.' Lauren stiffened, slightly defensive, because Mason knew her situation. 'But he'll need me. I always take care of him when he's ill. I can take him some fever medication and make him soup when he's feeling hungry.'

It was one of the things their mother had done, one of the roles Lauren had adopted.

'Lauren…' said Mason, gently, 'he's twenty years old. Don't you think he's capable of caring for himself?'

She flushed, aware that where Ben was concerned she had the tendency to be overprotective.

'Of course he is,' she huffed, 'but we all need someone sometimes.' She would do the same for Mason if he was sick.

Mason nodded, but looked unconvinced. 'Maybe he has friends who will check in with him, someone from the university? A girlfriend who's crazy enough about him that she'd risk catching whatever he has just to stroke his fevered brow.'

She winced, recalling the times when Mason had been ill and she'd gone around to his place anyway, just to see him and be there for him, and he'd done the same for her in return.

Lauren frowned, her heart thumping with uncertainty. 'He'd tell me if he had a girlfriend.' They were close. Ben confided in her…

'Would he?' asked Mason dubiously. 'It took me a long time to tell my parents about you, and that wasn't because I wasn't serious about you. I was, head over heels. It was because they were my parents, and it felt like none of their business.'

'Well, I'm not Ben's mother, so—'

'So stop acting like you are,' Mason implored. 'Call him, send him a care parcel, but don't change your plans for the entire weekend just because Ben has a cold.'

She shot him a look full of the indignation she felt. 'I don't know what you're saying.'

'I'm saying be what he needs, Laurie. Be his big sister.' He came to her, took both of her hands in his. 'But think about yourself too. Do what you want and need. Stop putting yourself last and making sacrifices that no one wants you to make.'

Lauren shook her head, trying to dislodge the irrational feeling that she'd done something wrong. 'I don't expect you to understand. Ben and I have a special bond. A unique relationship…'

Mason lifted her hands to his mouth and kissed the backs, one and then the other. 'And I love that you have each other to rely on and share things with, believe me.' His expression softened and he cupped her cheek. 'But don't you think rushing down to Wellington to hold Ben's hand is…a bit over the top? We'd made plans for this weekend. I was looking forward to spoiling you.'

A twinge of doubt pinched her ribs. 'I know and I'm sorry that I'm letting you down, but my family is important to me and—'

'And I'm not.' It wasn't a question. He stared, his only movement the slight tightening of his jaw.

'Of course I care about you, Mason. I just have other priorities too. I don't expect you to understand because you're an only child, but my mother would have wanted me to take care of my brother and that's what I've always done. You knew that about me when we met.'

If she'd thought he looked disappointed about the weekend, the defeat in his eyes then was hard to witness. 'We all have other priorities, Lauren, and I understand yours. I'd support you all the way, you know that. I'd even come with you to Wellington, just for the chance of spending a few minutes of this weekend with you in between your commitments to your brother. But relationships work both ways. You're giving me nothing in return and it feels awfully reminiscent of the last time you pulled away from us.'

She gasped, horrified that he'd throw up the past when they'd both confessed to making mistakes. 'We agreed that we both played a part in our break-up. You can't just blame me for everything.' Now, when she was one step away from loving him, and placing herself in the most vulnerable position of her adult life, he was changing the rules of the game.

He dropped her hands, turned away, snorted as if in disbelief. 'You know, I can't believe that I've done this again…'

'Done what?' Lauren's temples throbbed in confusion. Was what he'd said true? Lauren could admit that she probably had overreacted by rushing to buy a plane ticket, but were there deeper motives behind her actions? Was she spooked by how fast this was happening, by the force of her feelings for Mason this time around?

But he couldn't blame her for her caution. What did either of them know about making a serious relationship work?

'I might have been the one who left the country six years ago, but you're the one who ran away, from us, from what we could have had. You pushed me away, just like you're doing now.'

She shook her head as if she could shake the truth of his words from her consciousness, but he was right. She had pushed him away then, but she'd explained why, confessed her grief-driven doubts. Deep down, she'd known that he'd leave her anyway. People left. Her mother, Ben, Mason. What else was she supposed to do but protect herself?

'I'm not pushing you away.'

Her phone pinged; the ride share she'd ordered was outside.

She collected her bag from the bed and threw it over her shoulder, torn in so many directions she thought she might collapse into pieces on the ground.

He continued as if she hadn't spoken. 'Do you realise that you haven't even asked me if I got the consultant job?'

Lauren covered her mouth with her hand. 'Oh, I completely forgot. I'm so sorry. I got distracted.' She swallowed down her self-disgust, needing to get away from the way he was looking at her, but she had to ask.

'Did you get the job?'

He shook his head in disbelief, as if it was irrelevant. 'No.'

'I'm sorry,' she whispered, even more scared of what this meant for them.

'I don't want your apology, Lauren.' His expression grew tortured and a piece of her shrivelled. She didn't want to cause him pain, but she needed to be certain because last time she'd loved him they'd messed up, and another part of her had withered and died with grief.

She couldn't lose any more of herself to that emotion.

Numbness tingled in her fingers and toes. 'I don't know what else to say.' She was seconds away from crying, from spilling all of her past pain, her doubts and fears all over the front of his shirt in great heaving sobs.

The doorbell rang. They stared at each other for a few more seconds and then Lauren fired off a text to the driver. 'That's my ride.' She tried to swallow but her throat was too dry. 'I know I've made a big mess of things today, but I do want to make it right. Can I call you later? We can talk properly. Once I know that Ben is okay.'

He nodded, his expression resigned. 'Of course. I hope Ben recovers soon.'

She pressed her lips to his cheek and fled

to the taxi. She needed time to deal with her family stuff and then figure out how she felt. Because Mason deserved more than she'd been giving him and the last thing she wanted to do was hurt him again.

Slamming her front door behind him, Mason chased after Lauren, reaching her just as she opened the rear door of the taxi.

'Lauren!' he yelled, aware that he might be making the biggest mistake of his life, but driven by the urgency of letting her go once before without telling her exactly how he felt.

She turned, her wide eyes alarmed and red-rimmed.

He gripped her shoulders, hugged her close for a second and then held her at arm's length. 'I can't let you go without telling you this. I'm in love with you. There. I couldn't hold it in any longer.'

She looked up at him, overwhelmed, silent, and dread flushed his veins with ice.

'I know you're not ready to hear it,' he rushed on, 'but I didn't want us to part without you knowing how I feel. I planned a whole elaborate weekend so I could tell you properly this time, so you'd know and be in no doubt and perhaps then you'd be brave enough to tell me how you feel about me in return.'

Lauren clutched one hand to her chest as if in pain. 'Mason...' She shook her head and looked down at her feet. 'I have to go... My flight.'

He felt winded, shook his head in disbelief. 'I tell you I love you and you say nothing.'

Her eyes shone with unshed emotion. 'My head is full of worry for Ben. I need time to think.'

Deflated, his hands slid from her shoulders. 'Do you even care if there's an us, Lauren? You can't even give me that much of yourself, can you, not even this time around?'

'Of course I care. I've given you more of myself than I've ever given anyone else,' she whispered, hating how inadequate that sounded when spoken aloud. 'I'm sorry that I've let you down this weekend, I truly am, but—'

'But you're leaving anyway, just like that?' His heart sank at how far apart they still were emotionally. He loved her and she couldn't get away from him quick enough. History was repeating itself and yet again he would be the one to end up with a broken heart.

The driver muttered something over his shoulder and Lauren tossed her bag on the back seat. 'I have to go. I'm sorry.'

'I don't want your apology. I want you to

want me as much as I want you. I want more of you than you were willing to give me last time, but this—' he threw his arm out wide '—it feels like you're willing to give me even less, and I deserve more.'

Lauren nodded, tears filling her eyes. 'You do deserve more, Mason. You always have.'

Regardless of what he deserved, she left him anyway, speeding away, protecting her feelings once again. Only this time Mason was done.

# CHAPTER FOURTEEN

HOURS LATER, LAUREN EMERGED from the domestic terminal of Auckland Airport. Grady waved from the driver's seat of his car, which he'd pulled into the drop-off zone. Lauren sagged with relief and then sprinted towards the car, muttering an apology to the disgruntled-looking parking warden, who pointed at the *No Waiting* sign with an accusatory finger.

'I'm sorry. I'm here. Let's go,' she said, diving into the passenger seat and shoving her bag over her shoulder.

The minute she'd clicked her seatbelt into place, Grady pulled out. 'What's going on, Lauren?'

Lauren gripped her temples, her head hung low. 'I don't even know where to start. I'm a mess.' She couldn't cry again. She already had a headache from the tears she'd shed since the car had pulled away from Mason earlier.

Remembering her manners, she turned to her friend. 'Thanks so much for picking me up. I really appreciate it. You're a lifesaver.'

'No problem.' Grady frowned. 'You can pay me back by babysitting Molly some time.'

Lauren nodded and Grady wordlessly navigated the traffic for a few minutes. She fought the urge to consult her phone again for what felt like the millionth time, desperate to make the last ferry of the day to Waiheke Island.

'I'm confused,' he started up again when they were on the motorway heading into the city. 'First you fly to Wellington on a whim and then you turn straight around and fly back again, without even leaving the airport. Are you trying to use up all of your frequent flyer miles or something?'

She knew Grady was being kind, making light of her behaviour. But she only had one explanation for her erratic decision-making.

'Mason said he's in love with me,' she blurted. *And I love him too...*

The sickening words swirled in her head, because she'd been so confused by the intensity of her feelings for Mason, so terrified by the speed at which she'd fallen effortlessly back in love with him, that she'd overreacted to Ben's news, bungled their plans for the weekend and hurt Mason badly, the very last thing she'd wanted to do.

'So you ran away to Wellington?' Grady frowned but kept his eyes on the road.

'Yes. No. Kind of.' She covered her face with her hands, slowing down her panicked breathing. She had time to fix this. And she would, because she couldn't lose Mason a second time.

'I know… I messed up, big time,' she muttered, too scared to look at Grady's expression for confirmation that it was too late, that she'd already had too many chances. 'You have to help me make it right.' She gripped his arm and gave him a brief summary of the events of her morning, including her conversation with Mason and her whistlestop trip to Wellington Airport.

She hadn't even bothered telling Ben that she was in his city. Mason was right. He was a grown man. If he needed his big sister, he'd ask for her help. She'd really only freaked out, retreated to her comfort zone because she'd already been feeling out of control and overwhelmed by her feelings for Mason.

'I'll do what I can, but what's your plan?' Grady asked when they stopped at a set of traffic lights.

She groaned, banging her fist on the dashboard. 'I'm sick of plans. Overthinking, worrying about what might happen. That's what landed me in this mess in the first place. She'd had three hours to come up with some fail-safe strategy to win Mason back while she'd sat in Wellington waiting for a return flight, finally concluding that plans were grossly overrated.

'So for once in your life you don't have it all figured out?' Grady's voice bordered on incredulous.

'No,' she said, panic a hot ball in her chest. 'Can you drive any faster?'

'Nope,' Grady said. 'I'm not speeding and getting a ticket just because you've finally fallen in love.'

Lauren bit her fist in frustration. She'd always loved Mason. She'd probably never stopped loving him the first time around. She'd simply buried her pain alongside her grief for her mother and tried to live without him. But that wasn't living; that was hiding.

'Please can you just save the lecture and drop me at the ferry terminal? I'm going to Waiheke.'

'I hope that's where Mason is, because you need to tell him how you feel this time.'

'I will.' Lauren's legs began jiggling. 'At

least I hope that's where he is and that he's not already halfway across the Tasman.'

She'd called every hotel on the island, asking if they had a reservation for Mr Ward, until she'd tracked down his booking. He hadn't checked in yet, but his phone was switched off so this was her best shot. She couldn't just sit at home and wait; that would drive her crazy.

Now was definitely the time for action.

'I can't believe how badly I messed up,' she whispered, more hot achy tears finally spilling free.

Grady tilted a sympathetic smile her way. 'He'll understand if you explain how you feel about him. How do you feel? You do love him back, right?'

She nodded, searching his glove box for a tissue. 'I'm not sure that I ever stopped loving him, to be honest, not that he knows that. I was just so scared to feel anything that strong and intense after Mum died that instead I've spent most of my adult life pretending not to feel at all when it comes to my own life.'

'So what will you do when you find him?' Grady said. The fear in his voice shot panic through Lauren's veins.

'Beg him to give me another chance.' She gave up searching for a tissue and wiped her face on her sleeve. 'Follow him around until he can look at me with something other than disappointment. Pray that I haven't missed my opportunity.' She sniffed, her eyes stinging.

'Well, if he's disappointed, that's a good thing,' said Grady with the wisdom of an old soul. 'It means that he still cares.'

She dropped her head onto Grady's shoulder, grateful to have such a good friend.

Grady pressed his lips together in a grim line. 'Why didn't you tell me that you loved him then? If I'd known how you felt about each other I would have told you he'd called that time, broken my promise to him, encouraged you to go and find him.' He glanced sideways, regret haunting his stare.

'Please don't feel responsible in any way. If I'd realised how I felt about him at the time, I'd have hunted him down myself, don't worry. Instead I blocked him out. I'd already had years of practice, blocking out thoughts and happy memories of Mum, that by the time I pushed Mason away I'd one hundred percent convinced myself that it was for the best, that we would never have lasted, that I was saving myself from heartache down the road, when in reality all I was doing was drawing out the heartache over six long years.'

Her voice wobbled but she pushed on, finally certain of how she felt. 'To be honest, I'll probably always be an expert at hiding my deepest emotions, but reconnecting with Mason has shown me that there's more to fear from shielding my heart than there is from exposing it, being vulnerable. I don't want a hollow personal life. I want more. I want it all, with him, if he'll forgive me.'

She wanted to ride pillion on Mason's bike, feel the wind in her hair and his heat at her front. She wanted to skinny-dip with him and make out in public places and sleep in his arms on her wide-enough-for-two sofa. She wanted his love, even when she was terrified to lose it.

'Well, that's definitely worth getting a speeding fine for,' said Grady and he put his foot down.

# CHAPTER FIFTEEN

AFTER DRIVING HIS bike around Waiheke Island for most of the afternoon while he ruminated on what had transpired with Lauren, Mason pulled into the hotel he'd booked for their romantic getaway—a secluded boutique luxury lodge perched on the coast and boasting its own private beach.

The receptionist greeted him with a welcoming smile he struggled to return. He'd wanted to bring Lauren here. He'd planned to finally lay his feelings bare, to ask her to give them a second chance at a real committed relationship. He'd wanted to be upfront and honest with her, but she hadn't even given him the time of day, cutting him off, pushing him away and running, just like she'd done six years ago.

'Mason Ward. I have a reservation,' he said, wondering if Lauren had made it safely to Wellington. He should forget about her, not that that was a posibility. He hadn't managed it for the past six years so what made him think he could achieve it now?

The receptionist hesitated.

'The booking was for two people, but now it's just me.' He shrugged, sick to his stomach.

He'd told Lauren that he was in love with her, for goodness' sake, but even that hadn't made any difference. He'd even chased after her, this time determined not to give up as easily and always live with the regret. He was stronger than that.

The receptionist nodded and glanced over his shoulder. 'Yes. We're expecting you, Mr Ward, but there's…um…someone here to see you. She's been waiting a while.'

He turned around to find Lauren sitting near the fireplace. His heart lurched, part elation, part dread. Was she here to let him down again? To calmly rationalise all the reasons why they just wouldn't work out?

She stood, wordlessly twisting her hands in front of her, looking pale but still breathtakingly beautiful. Would he ever be free of loving her? He doubted it, but that didn't mean he'd continue to lay himself at her feet, only to be trampled on.

Mason absently accepted the room key

from the receptionist and crossed the foyer towards Lauren, his mind racing. How had she found him? Why wasn't she in Wellington? Was Ben okay?

He paused far enough away that he wouldn't be tempted to touch a single hair on her head, his natural inclination to take her in his arms and kiss her until she loved him the way he loved her.

'How did you know where to find me?' he said, pressure building in his head.

Lauren swallowed, her eyes dark pools of uncertainty. 'I called every hotel on the island until I got a hit. I didn't know that you'd be here for sure; I was just praying that you hadn't already gone back to Australia.'

He looked down at his feet in case the seed of hope that could germinate any second was clearly displayed on his face. 'No, not yet. I came here to consider my options.' He met her stare once more, recalling the promises he'd made to himself on the beach just thirty minutes ago. To walk away, whether it was going to Australia or another consultant position in New Zealand. Only now that she was standing in front of him, now that his heart recalled what was at stake, he couldn't seem to find one tenth of the resolve.

'What are you doing here Lauren?' he

asked bluntly, overwhelmed by her appearance and what it meant. He'd allowed her to hurt him once before, but he wasn't a fool.

'I wanted to apologise. I was crazy for leaving you earlier. I stupidly wasted several hours flying to Wellington and simply waiting in the airport for the next available return flight home.' She shook her head and rolled her eyes. 'I didn't even leave the airport.'

'Is Ben okay?' he asked.

'I don't know. I'm sure he's fine. I didn't tell him I was there. Look, can we talk?' She waved in the direction of the rear exit. 'There's a garden.'

He nodded, following her outside. They found a bench large enough that they wouldn't touch each other when they sat side by side in the landscaped garden beyond the hotel's restaurant. Mason wanted to reach across the divide that separated them so much that his hands shook. But he wanted to hear what she'd come all this way to say even more.

'I can't believe how badly I let you down this morning,' she whispered. 'I'm so sorry.'

Mason dragged his eyes away from the way her lips moved, forced himself to focus on the lamps that lit the walkway leading down to the hotel's private beach instead. 'I should have saved my grand declaration of love. You clearly needed space to visit your brother.' All he'd done was expose himself to more pain and rejection.

She shook her head. 'No. You've given me enough space. Six years of space. And I'm actually sorrier for myself, how I've let myself down.' She sat on the edge of the bench, impassioned. 'You told me that you loved me, Mason, something I've wanted to hear since our very first kiss that night on our beach, and I ruined that for myself and for you. Why?'

It was a rhetorical question because she gave him no time to answer.

'Because, all those years ago, I convinced myself that I wasn't ready. But I was just scared to love you, scared to have you love me in return, because I didn't want to lose you. But it happened anyway. I pushed you away before you could hurt me. I was a coward. And today I did it again.'

She stood, pacing a few feet away, her hands on her hips, anger and passion and fight rolling off her in waves. 'I don't think I fully realised how much we'd hurt each other last time until you showed up again. Nor did I fully acknowledge how in love with you I'd been then. All these years I've been pretending that I was okay, keeping busy, focusing on my work and my family in order to ignore what a mess my private life was. But I don't want to hide from it any more.'

She returned to stand before him, her eyes shining with unshed tears. 'I loved you six years ago, Mason, but what I feel now is bigger, stronger, un-survivable.' She placed her hand on her chest, her breath catching. 'I love you so much that it crushed me with terror. I felt that if we were to mess up again, to let each other down again…that I'd be broken beyond repair. So I panicked. I became all caught up in my own head. It felt easier to focus on Ben than on myself, on my own feelings for you—feelings I've been denying for weeks.'

She dragged in a breath as if collecting herself and he couldn't help the pride that stole his ability to speak. He'd always known she'd held back from fear; her mother's death had robbed her of the security to trust her feelings. But she was right. This time they had more power to hurt each other. They had to get it right.

'I'm going to book a room here. I'll give you all the time you need,' she said. 'But please give me a chance to make things right.' She backed up a pace, putting distance between them. 'Please know that the last thing I want this time is to push you away.' Another pace, so that she stepped onto the path that led back inside. 'Please don't leave us behind until you're certain of my love, even if you no longer want it.'

And then she was gone, leaving him with a decision to make and another hole punched in his chest.

Lauren was in the middle of a dream when she was jolted awake. Her neck cricked and she sat up in the armchair next to the fireplace, pain shooting to the base of her skull.

'Lauren, I've had enough time to think.' Mason loomed over her, dressed in the same clothes he'd worn when they'd walked in the garden.

'What time is it?' she asked, rubbing sleep from her gritty eyes.

'Two-fifteen. I thought you said you'd booked a room?' He straightened, his face etched with fatigue and his expression unreadable.

'There were no rooms available, so...' She'd decided to spend the night waiting in the foyer, only the heat from the huge fire in the hearth must have lured her into a fitful doze.

'We can't talk here. Come with me.' He collected Lauren's overnight bag from the floor, the one she'd packed to go to Wellington, and marched ahead along one of the guest corridors. Lauren hurried after him, her stomach a riot of fear and longing.

At the furthest door, he swiped a keycard and pushed inside the room, holding the door open for her.

'I'm sorry that I woke you, but I didn't want you to wait another six years for my decision.' He placed her bag on the floor just inside the room and Lauren had to grip the door handle at her back to stop herself from collapsing in a heap.

'I see.'

'Do you?' he asked, his burning eyes boring into hers. 'Because I don't think I've seen anything clearly since the first time I saw you at that lab where you stabbed at me as if I were a pincushion.'

In two strides he was in front of her, filling her vision, eclipsing any other consideration, being her everything.

'Mason…' she whispered, tears spilling free.

'No, Lauren. It's my turn to talk.' He cupped her face, his thumbs wiping at her tear tracks. 'I've wasted hours doing what you asked, thinking about what you said, and it's all irrelevant because I love you and I always have.'

'I love you too,' she snuffled against his chest, wetting his T-shirt.

'I know you do.' He stroked her hair, tilted up her chin, smiled indulgently. 'I've known all along. I was just too stupid, too scared to push the issue and make you admit it in case that backfired.' He placed his hand over hers on his chest, trapping it there over his thudding heart. 'But I felt it. You always showed me, even if you didn't say the words.'

He scooped a hand around the back of her neck and tucked her head against his steady but rapid heartbeat. 'When we were together last time, I was young, a bit messed-up, unsure of myself.' He pressed a kiss to the top of her head and Lauren squeezed his waist in case he changed his mind and disappeared.

'But I don't need the words. I just need you to feel my love and to trust it. Because I'll never give up on us again. I won't let you down. I won't walk away when things get tough, and they will. We're realists. We know every relationship has struggles. But you'll never have to fear my love ending, because I'll still love you from the grave. I'll love you eternally. And I'll show you every day for the rest of my life the truth of that.'

Fresh tears spilled onto her cheeks as she tried to drag in a full breath. He loved her. He believed she loved him.

Before she could draw another breath he cupped her face, brought her lips to his and kissed her and kissed her until her tears dried and her heart was so full she thought she might explode.

'Mason…' She pulled away, her eyes dry but puffy, her lips swollen from his kisses. 'I don't want to make another mistake. I want you to stay in Auckland or I'm coming with you to Australia. I want us to be together, see each other every day, fall asleep together every night.'

She lifted her face to his, looped her arms around his neck as their lips and tongues met in a passionate rush.

Mason gripped her waist and tumbled them backwards onto the bed. She sprawled on top of him, shoving at his T-shirt so she could press kisses over his chest, his neck, his jaw.

'I'm not going to Australia,' he said, his fingers gliding through her hair. 'I'm staying wherever you are.'

She grinned, her heart soaring. 'Good. Move into my house. Your rental is too far away from work, anyway.'

He grinned. 'Okay. Don't be bossy and demanding,' he teased.

'Why not?' she sighed, collapsing on top of him and nuzzling kisses up his neck. She wanted him now, naked, hers, for ever. 'I know what I want, and I've denied myself long enough. I want you. I want us. And I always have the last word.' She pressed her lips to his once more to silence any verbal retaliation.

Things turned purposeful, the bickering unnecessary as they showed each other the love they'd both finally declared.

# EPILOGUE

LAUREN STARED SO hard into Mason's eyes that her own stung. She didn't want to miss one second of his reaction as they made their vows to love each other for ever.

As was their way, they hadn't agreed on much when it had come to organising a wedding. Despite what Mason thought she should have, Lauren had wanted a quiet ceremony with just a handful of witnesses. Mason had vetoed a tux for beach casual attire and Lauren insisted on a band rather than a DJ. But one thing they had agreed on was that they would become man and wife on their beach, the site of all of their important moments: their first kiss, their first and only break-up, and Mason's proposal.

'Lauren and Mason,' their female celebrant said, 'you are now husband and wife.'

The small crowd gathered on the beach behind them cheered and clapped as Mason cupped Lauren's cheeks and she raised her face to his.

'I love you,' he said, looking down at her with his words also displayed in his stare.

'I love you too,' Lauren managed just before he closed the distance and sealed their union with a kiss.

Lauren clung to her new husband as if she'd never let him go. She sighed into their kiss. He looked so handsome in his white linen shirt and casual trousers. Lauren had chosen a simple ivory shift dress with spaghetti straps and flowers in her hair. Their feet were bare so they could feel the sand between their toes as they made a lifelong commitment to each other.

They finally broke apart, both of them unrepentant for the lengthy duration of their first kiss as a married couple. There would be plenty of time for hugs and congratulations from friends and family, but this time, these few precious seconds of celebration, was for them.

'Allow my sister up for air,' laughed Ben, slapping Mason on the shoulder so he could embrace Lauren in a six-foot-three bear hug. As her man of honour, he too looked handsome enough to bring tears to Lauren's eyes. Her father was next with hugs and congratulations, followed by Grady, her second man of honour.

Champagne corks popped and glasses were passed around to the guests. The photographer appeared but, before they could become too caught up in the celebrations, Lauren took Mason's hand and led him along the water's edge, away from the wedding party.

'Are you okay, Mrs Ward?' he asked when they were alone, raising her hand to his lips and pressing a kiss over her shiny new gold band.

'That's Dr Ward to you, and I'm better than okay. I just wanted a few minutes alone with my husband.' She paused, pulled him close for a kiss and sighed. 'I don't think I'll ever take those two words for granted: my husband.'

'I feel the same about *my wife*.'

Lauren smiled, her chest tight with happiness. She clung to his hand and rested her head against his shoulder as they walked a little further. 'I can't wait for our honeymoon. I hope you had a hearty breakfast, because you're going to need the stamina. I might not let you out of our hotel room for a month.'

Mason chuckled. 'But what about Europe? We have all that sightseeing to do.'

They'd booked a month-long tour of Europe's main cities and tourist spots, followed by a six-month working sabbatical in London, Mason in the surgical department and Lauren in Accident and Emergency.

'Sightseeing is overrated,' said Lauren in all seriousness. 'I have everything I'll ever need right here.' She looked down at their clasped hands, their entwined fingers, and then lifted his other hand to her lips, kissing his wedding band in a repeat of his gesture.

'Are you saying you've changed your mind about our sabbatical?' he asked with a wink. 'Because there are going to be two very disgruntled departments in London if we don't show up for work next month.'

'I suppose I can muddle through, as long as you're by my side.'

'You'll always have that.' He gripped her hips and pressed her body flush with his.

'Yeah? Promise?' She wrapped her arms around his waist and held him close.

'Absolutely.'

'Promise me one more thing…' she said.

'Anything.' He pulled back, kissed the end of her nose and then her lips. 'Anything at all.'

'Later, when the reception is over and that lot have gone home—' she tilted her head towards their friends and family '—promise me that we can jump on the bike, come back here and go for a midnight swim.'

'Brilliant plan,' he said, his eyes heating. 'As long as we can go skinny-dipping.'

Lauren grinned, already wishing away the rest of her wedding day so she could be alone with Mason.

They sealed the deal with a kiss.

* * * * *

*Look out for the next story in the*
*Gulf Harbor ER duet*

Breaking the Single Mom's Rules

*If you enjoyed this story, check out*
*these other great reads from*
*JC Harroway*

How to Resist the Single Dad
Forbidden Fling with Dr. Right
Tempting the Enemy

*All available now!*